The Flash Project:

A Film Writer's Journey into Literary Flash Fiction

By Todd Fabyanic

Table of Contents

Introduction

This book is a compilation of several flash fiction and short stories. Written in my college years at Full Sail University, Orlando, Florida. I 've always been attracted to the entertainment industry (Films, Music, Theater). When I was young I wanted to be a star (Music/Actor/Celebrity). One day I decided to try, and guess what, I actually got the part. I realized I was not able to memorize lines (My flaw). This led me to my true desire, and this is where I found my true calling: A Writer. I wanted to create stories, and I wanted to create movies. Yes, I am a dreamer, it's who I am, and who I have always been. I remember riding in a car with my father when I was young. I asked a hundred questions about something. My dad looked at me and asked, "Are you writing a book?" 43 years later, I called him and told him, "Yes, I am writing a book (LOL)." I finally found my true calling and purpose. I wish it hadn't taken me 45 years to get here, but that's ok. There is still plenty of time to fulfill my purpose.

I decided to go to college. I knew nothing about writing, accept the ideas I had in my head. It was time to make those thoughts a reality. I learned about genres of writing (diction/vocabulary, style, prompts, and niches to name a few). I published this book (Also part of the course). I collaboration of my writing (Stories) into one book/eBook.

Throughout the school term, it was available via eBook, digital version only. After school (Once finished), it became available for print. I was pleased with the work. Full Sail University was a fantastic school. Flash Fiction was not what I intended when I started my journey. I went to school to become a film writer. That's why I titled this book, *"A film writer's journey into literary flash fiction."*

I found love and respect for the art of flash fiction, and the style of writing. Flash fiction helps me write out storylines. Fast and easy outlines for all those ideas pounding my head. I have great respect for my professors, and other writers (Professional & Freelance). They have been so helpful and patient with me.. A very special thanks to all of you. I hope you enjoy this book. . Thank you all so much.

Todd Fabyanic

Everything Revolves Around the Dance Floor

Tonight's the night, and everyone just got paid. The front door opens, and partygoers enter the club. They take their seats and find good spots at the bar. Hi-fives, hugs, and handshakes are all to be seen from wall to wall. I dim the house lights and turn on the chasers. Red, blue, and yellow lights flow through the purple blacklight lit main room. Late at night when all is done, I close my eyes, I still see those purple black lights as my eyes re-adjust before I go to sleep.

I turn on the little DJ light in my booth for eye balance, but I still keep the space dark. The audience knows I am about to begin. "Turn it up," Someone shouts. Before I play the first song, I ask myself, to whom do I play first? Is it the crowd? Is it the staff or management? Is it the girls or is it the guys? Is it myself? I like to remember my training and experience before I begin every shift. There is one thing I have told myself from day one, "Everything revolves around the dance floor."

Playing to management or a manager is always recommended because it provides job security, especially for a house DJ (Disc Jockey). If the boss likes you, he will want to keep you around. Usually, management (or your boss) will tell you songs they enjoy when you are or were hired, or when they open up to you after they like you (or your style). I've always taken notes of these song requests. Therefore, I put two of my boss's favorite songs into my special playlist queue.

I look around the room (read the room) and ask myself, is my boss on the floor or in their office? You don't want to play their song if they're in the office. Sure, they might dance around their paperwork, but the main room will have no effect. It is best to play a manager's song when they are present in the room. This way: they get excited in front of the guests which creates an effect in the room. Plus, the guests in the club always want to befriend management. This makes them feel special, and it should. This effect makes them feel welcome here.

Maybe I should play to the staff. A bartender can make or break a night. Nobody wants an upset bartender to spread bad vibes all night long. Bartenders love it when the DJ plays their jam, 'Gets em' every time.' When the bartender's happy, it creates good energy in the room–– Usually 'shout outs' to the DJ, or the annoying ringing of a bell behind the bar. But hey! It's all good baby, baby.

Catering to requested songs works for staff members as well. The doorman can get hyped up and create a fun experience for guests at the door as they enter the scene. A waitress can get so excited, that it arouses the guests (not just the guys, girls just want to have fun, too). Who doesn't want those pretty ladies to be happy? Happy ladies; make happy dudes: That's a fact. Bouncers (security staff members) are more friendly to guests when they enjoy the music. This makes the guest feel comfortable, and not like they're in a hostile environment. Excitement is what the people come to experience. So I ask myself, is it time for a staff drop? Unfortunately, not yet... the night is still young. The bartender and staff are occupied greeting guests. Therefore, energy is already in the room, and it's best to never disturb flowing energy. So I will put staff picks (song requests) in my special playlist queue for later on. When the welcome energy dies, and the room needs a pick-me-up, that's when I will play some staff drops.

The only guest left to cater to... is the crowd. Should I play a girly song for the ladies, or a masculine song for the fellas (guys)? What style? Is this a Rock, Pop, Rap, Latin, Country, or Techno (EDM) crowd? Do they want mainstream top 40 radio hits, or underground (Indie) music? The night is young... I could start with some brand-new songs to introduce the crowd too. Dance Tip 101: Never play a breaking new song (no one knows) on a crowded dance floor. It's not that they don't like it, it's just they don't know it. Ten times out of ten, they will stop dancing to listen to the song, and that means you will have to work really hard for the next two to three songs to get them to dance again. Everything revolves around the dance floor. The dance floor is always the top priority in any scene, at any venue. If people dance, they're having fun. Even the people watching, is what they come to experience. Do you want to go to a club of just people sitting around, that's what lounges are for, and dive bars are for getting tipsy. Clubs are for dancing. All eyes turn to the dance floor, the true sign of any party. If the dance floor is rockin'–– the DJ is knockin' (Good DJ). Everything revolves around the dance floor.

It's not as easy as you think to get the dance going, it takes build-up. First, we start with a few radio hits or hit songs people like (and know). Background hits! The kind of music you can enjoy while you walk around and greet your friends. Then, turn it up a notch. Maybe play a new hit, but not the jam, not yet. This will get the audience members playing around. They start to move or make little dance jesters as they mingle. The perfect spot to play some requests from staff members and management. Everyone in the club is enjoying the vibe and reacting to the playlist. Take a couple requests from guests. Oh God! Please–– no terrible songs or slow stuff, and that's putting it nicely. Remember, everyone in the club (for some odd reason) thinks they're the DJ. Note: "I'm a DJ, not a jukebox." But I do my best.

The night flows from mainstream radio play to upbeat hits, and finally, someone hits the dance floor. I go to my, 'Uptime Playlist.' Now, I break out the jams, if it's not too early. I have two upbeat lists, just in case they dance too early. This saves the best songs for the grand finale (usually midnight to close). The night is a hit, and everyone just got paid. I read the room and work the dance floor. I go around the room (read the crowd) and play various music to each guest's taste as I watch them from my DJ booth.

The beautiful waitress approaches my DJ booth. She walks up and shouts, "Time for last call." I swear, it happens every time!

The Porch Light

Who was I but just an ordinary man trying to live a moderate life, or at least I once was. I never asked for any of this. In this family, blood is thicker than mud. When mud dries, it turns hard as stone. Best be careful, because If you're not, solid rock can shatter into a million pieces. I was happy with clay. You can do a lot of things with clay, wet or dry. My guess is you wouldn't know anything about that... now would you? Maybe it's best if I tell you my story. Maybe then, you'll have a better understanding of my situation.

My name is John Marlowe. *That's right!* As you probably already guessed, I am the only living son of Eddie Marlowe, Godfather of the Marlowe family. My family has been running the show in Boston since the great depression. Mostly East Arlington, but from Arlington to Davis Square–– everybody knows you don't mess with Marlowe. *That's not advice, just wise words around these parts, fellow.* Even if my Family has always been what you might call, convivial.

Man! I tell you... my life was simple. I had it, what you call... good! I finished my schooling and became a mechanic. Nothing fancy like an airline mechanic–– not even sports cars. *Nope!* I was just your everyday mechanic busting my hump at the local Jiffy Lube. I earned everything I had and was able to keep up with the bills. *God Bless the USA; I love this country.* I didn't have to do anything my father did. I was free, and most of all... loving every second of it. I was living the real American dream.

One day I received a call that my father passed. *No! He wasn't killed. Everybody loved that man.* He wasn't a thug-head like them other gangsters. He treated the family business like a businessman. He did everything he could to help people. *Always business, only business. If it wasn't business, then here... have a drink and take a seat.* That was my old man.

I guess it was age that finally caught up to the old man. He kicked the bucket on the front porch. No one even knew he was dead until mourning. He had sat there in his chair, on the front porch, under the porch light, all night long. No one thought anything of it. They said a garbage man noticed him and asked where he wanted to place the empty cans. The garbage man noticed his lifelessness and called it in. Later that day, I got the call. When I received the call, I packed my suitcase and caught the first train out of Philly. The 2:30pm train from Philly to Boston was about a six-hour phlegmatic ride.

When I arrived in Boston, Toad was waiting for me at the station. We gave him that name because he was toady, one who flatters in hope of gaining favors. Overall, Toad was a good guy, just always looking for a way-up. Toad was the perfect example of everything I ran away from since the day I hit-the-door to become a mechanic. I didn't want to chase that life, I wanted to escape it.

Toad drove me to the house and showed me were they found my father. The more Toad comforted me, the more I wondered what he was expecting. Toad never opened up to me this way before, I didn't quite know how to take it, but I was grateful he was there.

The next morning we held the funeral and buried my father. *R.I.P. Eddie Marlowe, Godfather of the Marlowe family.* Everyone showed up to express their condolences. No one; not a single person, not even the higher-ups (bosses from other cities) said a single word about business. Deep inside, I knew they were wondering who was going to become Arlington's new Made-Man.

I had no desire to step up, but I loved my father. I respected the way he chose to run his business. I knew he did what he had to do (when he had to do it), but I also knew my father always did everything in his power to result things... peacefully and professionally. He always tried to help people. He was not like those thugs and heartless cruel mobsters who only care about the money and power. My dad had heart, and everyone knew it. *Silent as 4:30am that funeral service was.*

After the funeral we all had a nice dinner together, and many toast in honor of my father. Some people gave speeches, and others told stories. A couple laughs and a few tears, but mostly great memories. I knew most of the stories because I grew up in that house. There were no strangers in my house that day, except my father's attorney. I had never met him before. He respectfully approached me privately after dinner. He said, "Out of respect... we'll talk later. Expect me soon."

The next morning: the doorbell rang. The attorney was at the front door with three of the four kings (big bosses) behind him. My father's business partners. My father was the fourth king, and since he passed there were only three kings left. My father loved his relationship with kings. I opened the door and showed the men into my father's office room. The attorney sat down at the desk and began to open his briefcase. Two of the three kings took a seat at the round side-table. They opened the old man's liquor cabinet and poured themselves a drink. The third king stood by the window looking out. "Do you know your porch light is on?" he asked.

I looked out the office window. "That's strange," I uttered. I didn't turn it on. Then again, maybe I forgot, I thought myself. I chose to think nothing of it and just laughed. I turned around to the two kings drinking Pop's good liquor, "You guys better be careful... Pop's a watching." We all had a good laugh. The last laugh before my life completely changed forever. It was there, in that room, in that moment, that my life changed forever.

The attorney pulled out my father's will and placed it on the desk. He flipped through the papers and signed a couple of them. "Your father has bestowed his entire belongings unto you. The house, his bank accounts, and his business... all goes to you. If you will just sign right here, I will be on my way... and I think these gentlemen would like to have a word with you."

"If they shoot me... you're my only witness," I shouted abruptly.

The room got quite, cold, and oddly still. A midday cloud darkened the office. The kings looked at me as if they were totally offended. I looked right back and held my straight face. Looking each one in the eye as I glanced around the room. Then, I just busted out laughing. The Kings laughed too. I signed the papers, and the attorney left the office.

It was just me and the kings, all alone. I had never been alone with them before. "you guys know I was just kidding about the whole... shoot me thing," I mentioned as they taunted me with their wondering, playful, get-me-back stillness. "My dad loved you guys. He always spoke very highly of each and every single one of you." *I just had to throw that in.* "If you're here about the business, I have no problem selling. My father would be pleased, and I can get back to my life. All I ask... is for a fare offer... in honor of my father... may he rest in peace."

"Careful! Pop's a watching, kid." The king standing by the window said, as he stared at the porch light. The day-cloud above moved, and the sun lit the room again. He closed the window curtain, "I think we have other intentions." He boldly turned around and suggested, "Let's make Pop proud."

I almost swallowed my tongue as I mentioned, "Whatever your intentions may be... I think you'll find me very cooperative."

"Good!" The king in the chair said, with his brandy funneling around in his cheerful hand. "We have decided... correction... we think it's best... if you stay awhile.. Get a taste before you make a decision. This would be best for everybody."

Life changing! I know... See, I told you my life was about to change, but this was only just the beginning. *C'mon! Let's be honest.* You can't say no to the Kings. 'Three they may be - even without four - once you say no - in their presence, you will stand no more.' *Everybody knows that.*

Just like that: it was done, and I was a Made-Man. I never asked for any of this. Do you understand my situation now? *Good!* As you naturally guessed, I stepped up and filled my father's shoes. When the kings left I went to turn off the porch light, but it was already turned off. 'Maybe one of the kings turned it off,' I thought.

Later, Toad came to visit me. "Shout-outs to the new big guy," He shouted as he hung his jacket on the coat hanger. "I'm here for you. Anything you need... boss." That was Toad, always looking for opportunity. I have got to give the guy credit; he does live up to his name. *Not all do!* I decided to make Toad's day. *I trusted him, (after-all) we came up together*. I promoted Toad to my right-hand man, and he took the position. I asked him if I could trust him?

"With your very life, Don... wait! Is it Don Marlowe, or Don John?" He asked.

"Don John... I like that."

"Yes, sir! Don... John. Consider me your new... Right. Now! Slap me in my face and make this official."

I gave him a love-tap oh his cheek (like my father did). He stood so proud. I never understood any of It, but who am I to judge anyone... who doesn't owe me money. That was the family business... loans. We lent money to people who the banks, or '*The System,*' refused to acknowledge. That's why everyone loved my father. Not just the money, but the fact my father never took advantage of them. He gave people a fare-shot, and a honest handshake deal. His rates were reasonable as his terms.

The Marlowe Terms and Conditions contract: as long as the family is invested, the family attended to it's investment. This meant Marlowe business associates would be present and granted access to the client's business until the loan was paid back in full. *A deal's a deal!*

Most thugs and mobsters set-up shops in other people's businesses (Usually backrooms), but not my father, he let the clients run their businesses as they wish. He even supported them. They could always rely on him, and Pop was happy to help if he could. He still audited their books to keep them honest. Pop's was professional about it and gave the clients respect. His policy was honesty, just be honest and he would work with you. He wanted to see people succeed.

He also provided security services and protection to his clients. Everyone knew, if you mess with Marlowe business, it will not end well. That's the only part of business that gangsters, thugs, and really– really bad dudes came into play. "The only acceptation," my father would say. Even then, he tried to work it out. *Maybe, because he knew how it would end.* My father was not a violent man. He despised violence, but even he knew that this business had many faces.

Speaking of mobsters, thugs, and goons: it was around this time on the north-east side of Arlington, Gino Vanelli was plotting his move. He was planning to assassinate me, and name himself the new Don. Gino was a thug, and he was no joke. *My life was in grave danger.* With Pop gone, the men would look for leadership. Whispers, rumors, gossip, and concerns began to be spoken in shadows. Soon, I would have to deal with Gino Vanelli.

I had no clue of Gino's deceptions, but every sign was telling me to watch out. One afternoon, Gino came to pay me a visit. He entered my house and sat down in the hall. He sat quietly with no expression on his face. Like a soldier standing guard, he just stared at the wall. Finally, I called him into my office.

Toad and I were discussing; or should I say, considering extending loans to help people. Gino expressed his disagreement. He stated, "They agreed to the terms when they signed for the loans." He was persistent in expressing his point of view.

The porch light caught my eye, as Gino stood firm and heartless in my office. "Who turned on the porch light," I shouted as I stood up. I rushed out of my office towards the front door. I noticed the light switch was turned off, but the porch light was on. I flipped the switch, but the light stayed on. 'I must be going mad,' I thought to myself.

I noticed Gino and Toad standing behind me, so I played it cool. I turned around to address them. "Let me think this over, then we will decide." I tried best to acknowledge Gino's point of view. 'Gino! You do make a point, but I have every intension of living up to my father's standards. That's what he would want, and he did... leave this business to me to carry on." I shook Gino's hand respectfully and wished him well.

I should have known right there by the look on Gino's face, that he was not to be trusted. *Hard to read... that Gino Vanelli is.* You never know what that nutcase is thinking. All I can tell you is, Don't underestimate Gino for one second. As Gino left, the porch light turned off.

"I'm going to fix that light," I uttered as I walked to the garage to fetch my toolbox. "Either I'm nuts, or that porch light is broken." Thank God no one heard me talking to myself. *That would not sit well with these guys.* That porch light was driving me mad, so I opened the switch panel, but I found nothing wrong. *Nothing! Nadda!*

Later that night, I decided to skim through some debt-files in my office. I placed two wooden paper-crates on my desk. One crate for yes (Approve extension loans). The other crate was for no (Do not extend loans). The first file was a man named Elton. When I opened his file the porch light came on. The porch light made me think of Pop. I remembered Elton was one of my father's favorite clients. 'Maybe the porch light's a sign,' I thought. I remembered Pop telling me, "Always pay attention to detail." I placed Elton's file into the yes pile.

I picked up a second file. The file belonged to man named Craig. The porch light turned off. Craig had dealt deceitfully with my father. I can't count the times my father said he couldn't wait to be done with Craig. Thankfully for me, Craig was close to ending his deal. I happily placed Craig's file into the... do not extend pile.

When I picked up the third file, I was suddenly surprised... it was Toad's file. I never knew Toad was in debt to my family. I was appalled.

So appalled that I skimmed the file thoroughly. I noticed Toad was good on his payments. The porch light came on. This time, I knew it was a sign. I pulled my stamper out and decided to consolidate Toad's debt. As I was putting away the file, Toad walked into my office. He recognized the file in my hand.

"I was going to tell you sooner, but I figured you would find out eventually," Toad said in a soft sincere tone. "For the record, I never tried to deceive you. I have every intention of paying off that loan."

I told Toad, "Don't worry about it. I closed the book out."

"Don't you dare," He stated with a firm tone. "I borrowed. I'll pay."

"Why?" I asked. I also asked Toad to tell me what happened.

He said, "I took a shot. In the end... It's as if the horse to win tripped and fell... and ended up disqualified. That said, it was still a good move. Besides... it made me a better man."

"Do explain," I Inquired.

Toad shuffled around my office as he explained. "Now I know what it's like to do everything you can, and no matter how hard you try, it all fails. I never understood that until now. They don't call me Toad for no reason. I took my shot just like the people in those files. Some work out, and some don't. Your father knew that. And now, I understand what he meant. It made me a better man."

The porch light turned off. I stepped over to the window. As I looked out, Toad asked me what I was looking at. He even reached for his pistol to protect me. I told him to calm down and explained the whole porch light scenario. He took it rather well, but we both agreed it was best kept secret. Toad found the porch light situation intriguing. He asked me a few questions.

"When was the first time, the light came on?" He asked.

"The moment I signed the attorney's papers," I answered.

"And to whom?" he inquired very suspiciously.

I sat down at my desk chair. I began to reminisce, "Let's see... there was... the kings, some of the men, these files, Oh! And Gino."

"Maybe Pops is trying to tell you something," he uttered. Then Toad paused. He closed the window curtains and whispered to me, "You better watch out for that guy."

"Do tell," I insisted.

"This stays between you and I, John. Whispers floating in the wind say Gino wants to kill you. He wants to take that seat for himself. Many men are loyal to him, and he has earned their respect. The good news is that most of the men are still loyal to your father. They want to see what you do before they make any decisions. You can sleep comfortably... for now, but eventually... the men in this town, will see the truth. I can assure you... that."

I appreciated Toad's honesty. He saved my life that night (whether he knew it or not). I'll never forget his last words to me that night. "No matter what happens... or whichever way this goes... I'm with you, John!"

Toad was right, Gino Vanelli was plotting against me. All week long I noticed my men divided. Some were loyal, but others were skeptic. There was split amongst the family. I witnessed groups forming.

Eventually, I found Gino's flaw. It was Tony Giovanni. I noticed Tony hanging around the wrong crowd in the split. My father saved his very worthless life, and I did not hesitate for one second to remind him of that fact when I called him into my office privately. *Tony Giovanni broke like a fine wine glass hitting an interior marbled floor.*

"Gino plans to take you out," Tony Spewed. "He plans to get-the-drop-on-you Friday, on the money run." Tony gave me some very special insight. "Nobody outside knows, but everyone inside knows this week's run will be huge. If they find you dead with that amount of cash, people might assume you're on the take... and assume you're not like your father. That's where Gino plans to play hero. Step-in and save the business from your most unfortunate accident." *Sang like a cannery, Tony did.*

I asked Tony, "And where does Gino plan to get me?" *Like a boss!*

Tony told me everything. "In between the bank and dock house. Gino wants you to be found. He will make his move in the very Tigris eye of the general public."

"What about the money?" I asked. *Like a boss!*

"Gino doesn't care about the money. Once he's in charge, the money will come."

Tony was correct, I didn't know Gino was smart enough to figure that out. *Maybe I underestimated that sneaky little snake, Gino.* The porch light came on, and I noticed it secretly. I kept my promise to Tony and granted him safe passage. No one was to harm Tony, he had proven his loyalty and told me the truth. *Besides, I knew now... what Gino was really up too.* The only question left was, What was I going to do about it? When Tony left, the porch light turned off.

Thursday night I stayed awake in my office half the night. Every time I came up with a plan I would look to the porch light. *Nothing! Nadda! Not even a flicker.* I remembered my father telling me (<u>Words of (Pop's) Wisdom</u>), "*Life will test you. If you don't pass the first test, you never will. If you break your own rules, even once, you'll do it again and again and yet again. It means you have no foundation, and foundation is a man's structure. Without it... the building crumbles. Life will test you to see what you do, but it's the first test that matters most, kid.*" The porch light came on, but I already knew what I had to do.

Friday morning (money run day). I called an emergency meeting in my office. *This would throw off any suspicions. Holding a gathering on a business day such as this, would be considered standard procedure.* The meeting was only amongst the men I trusted. None of Gino's men were present, except Niko. I knew Niko was spying for Gino, and I used it to my advantage. I told some little white lies of dis-information in the presence of Niko. After Niko left, I told my men the truth. I did not lie to my loyal men; I told them the whole shoot-bang-kaboodle. *They understood.* Everyone knew exactly what to do, when we left the house to make the money run.

I got into my car and told the driver to hold-up before we drove off. I looked at the porch. The porch light flickered (It was a sign). Then, we pulled out of the driveway and headed to the bank on Main St.

<u>Marlowe Money Run (Instructions)</u>: Deposit the legit loan payment money into the bank. Separate the interest (Marlowe profit) money into carrier bags. Take the money bags to our safe house and put the money into the safe. The safe house is located in a warehouse by the docks, we call this location, The Dock House. This is how the Marlowe family has run the organization since the great depression. We lost faith in banks after the bank-runs. The Marlowe's learned how to diversify its vast economic equity.

On Main Street, we stopped at the bank. Everything went according to plan. We secretly switched the money into another unmarked van. The money car was a trap for Gino. *He had no clue what he was about to walk into.* Once the money car cleared, we sent the second unmarked van to another stash house out in the countryside. *We'll get it later, it's safe there... for now.* I crawled into the trunk of a Lincoln town car. All three vehicles went three separate ways. Everything went smooth. *Perfect as planned.*

At approximately 3:37pm, at the intersection of Massachusetts Ave. & Mill St. (a couple blocks north of the bank), Gino and his goons hit the money car. Gino had gunmen on the rooftops of the Butternut Bakehouse. From Mill St. to Ramsdell Ct. the small city street block was a hen hunt ambush. Gino's men unloaded everything they had at the truck. The driver was safe up front because it was bulletproof armored, but the back is where I was supposed to be. *It was as thin as a tin can.* The bullets ripped through the sheet metal of the back end and tore it to shreds. The money car burst into flames. The driver stopped the vehicle and fled. Gino's men let him go and focused on the area I was supposed to be. They opened fire until the money car exploded.

Gino was close-by. He watched from the café diner next to the shoe repair store. He could see everything, except for the goons I sent into the backdoor. Gino was so focused on watching all of the action, he took his eyes off the backdoor. My guys crept in quietly, and when it was over, Gino turned around to a big surprise... My guys, at gun point.

Gino had no back-up. Every man under his command was on the rooftop, and probably fleeing the scene by this point. Gino was wide open, and my guys took him. They tied Gino up and put him into a special delivery truck I arranged just for him. I don't know how cozy he was in that truck, but I do know, he had no idea about the surprise party we planned.

The truck pulled-up to the Dock House on Mystic Valley Pkwy, right across the street from the Mr. Pleasant Cemetery. They pulled Gino out of the truck and tied him to a chair in the Dock House. *I wanted Gino to see everything.* The look on his face when my men walked into the dock house; especially, the men who were supposed to be in the back of that money car. *Like witnessing dead men walking right atchya!* Still, Gino's face was cold. Like a soldier, he didn't even flinch... until I walked in.

I didn't walk-in the same entrance as my men. *No!* I came-in through the office. *The big boss office door is how I made my entrance.* The look on Gino's face when I walked in. He knew he was about to be swimming with the fishes. *This face: he could not hide.* I never saw Gino break a sweat, until that moment. I had my men place a table between Gino and me. I grabbed a chair, a nice comfortable office chair with fine linen. Gino and I sat at that table in the Dock House. A long, cold, deadly firm-face stare.

"Let's just get this over with," Gino said.

"If that's what you wish," I replied as I stared Gino up and down. All I could hear was my father's voice in my head, *'Life will test you, Kid.'*

As I sat there, I suddenly realized the porch light wasn't telling me what I thought it was. The porch light was getting my attention to focus on the details. The porch light first lit up with the three kings. *'It all made sense now.'* The kings didn't accept my offer because they knew Gino was a problem. Next, the light came on for Toad, but I didn't notice until that night in my office. Toad told me of Gino's deception. The porch light made me alert to Toad's warning. On top of that, The light was only turning on when I picked up files of people my father trusted. The very insight I used to select the men I trusted on the money run. Each man in the room was attached to one of the files that light up the porch light. *Not one man in that room, betrayed me.* In the end, I used the porch light to confirm my plan of action. On the morning of the run, I refused to leave until the porch light confirmed. That porch light had a say in everything... all of it!

"Well! Are you going to kill me... or what?" Gino shouted.

"That's up to you, Gino."

"What do you mean? That's up to me."

"I could kill you; God knows you deserve it. Instead, How about if I make you an offer?'

Confused; Gino paused. Then he asked, "What offer?"

"The deal of your life, Gino. I know, when I made Toad my right... that hurt you. Maybe I overlooked somethings. I must say, you have proven yourself capable of... things I might need done. Like dealing with guys like you. How about... instead of killing you... I... Promote you."

"What?" Gino shouted hysterically.

"I thought of a new position. I call it... My left-hand man. Would you like to be my left?"

"What's that?" Gino asked.

"Well, Toad's my right. He can take care of all my good business. When things go well, Toad can handle it. But... when things don't go so well... maybe... that's when you step-in and take care of the situation. I'm offering you everything you ever wanted. Being my left is big deal.

You get the promotion, the pay bump, the name, power, and even the respect. That is what you want... isn't it?"

Gino answered, "Yeah! That's what I want."

I sympathized with Gino rationally. "I'm sorry I didn't recognize you at first. Well... with my father's funeral and everything, I'm sure you can understand if it took me a minute to realize your value."

Gino started to become, convinced. He really opened-up to me. "I guess so, but after today, how can you or anybody forgive me after doing a thing like that?"

"Peanuts, Gino. All you did was blow up an empty truck. Of course... you did open-up on Main Street, but that's nothing a little wealth spreading can't fix. No one got hurt, Gino." I looked around the Dock House. My men were shocked by my gesture to Gino. "We just had a little misunderstanding... Right guys?" My men all nodded. "Happens all the time. Besides, If I lose you, who will take care of things... that need taken care of? I'm willing to let bygones be bygones. Bury the hatchet, as they say."

Gino began to nod his head. "You want me to be your left?"

"Yes! When something goes left... You have my full authority to deal with it... by any means... you feel necessary. You have my word."

I looked Gino right in his dead cold killer eyes. "I never wanted any of this. But you... Toad... and all you guys... do. I see now. And I see that you take this life very serious... and I apologize if I didn't see that before. I promise you... No... I promise all of you guys. From this day forward... as your Don... I will always take care of this family. All of you! All of us! The Marlowe Family; one big happy family. I Promise."

Grown men wept as they grabbed their handkerchiefs. *The nose blowing was excruciating.* In that room of non-believers, I made believers out of each and every single one of them... even Gino. He accepted my offer and we decided to make immense of the whole situation. No one had ever seen anything like it, A don forgiving an assassination attempt. *Not even my father himself, had done such a heartful move.*

From that day on, The Marlowe family was reunited under two columns. The right column (The good workers), and the left column (those who ain't afraid to get their hands dirty). It was understood that all jobs were essential, and no man was above or below anyone else. Some say I created my first slogan that day, *If you can't beat em'... buy em'.*

Later that evening; I returned home to find the porch light shining brighter than ever. I walked-up to the porch and stood under its radiant glow. The porch light shined so bright, it shattered and broke into pieces. I grabbed a broom and dust pan from the hallway. As I was sweeping up the shattered glass, something came over me. I realized Pop's work was done. I looked up to the sky and said, "Thanks Pop! I'll take it from here."

One Last thing (Before You Go)

They say a father's work is never done, but apparently a dad's job comes with a due date. I'll never forget that hot summer day in southern Florida as I prepared to have one last talk with my daughter before I let her go out into this world with her father's love and blessing. I checked into some old do-drop-in hotel on the strip. I paid for the night, but I only needed the place for less than an hour. The place had that signature retro vintage look. It had pin striped sheets on the beds, freshly vacuumed dark rug carpet, and it even had one of those old-time wired phones. I don't even think people use carpeted walls anymore. The decor fixtures were pieces of art, as the wall lamps hung beautifully over each bed. The patio was my choice.

(Ding Dong)

The doorbell rang and I knew it was her. She had arrived, at least. My nerves were so spun, I felt fuzzy all over. I took a deep breath to calm myself before I opened that door. "Hey dad," she said as she wrapped her arms around me, squeezing me. I wished she'd never let go. "I can't believe you're actually here." She smiled. "Where's mom? Is she here?" she asked.

"No, mom is not here," I told her. "This is just for me and you." My hands were beginning to sweat, I was so nervous. "Let's talk on the patio. I know you're busy. Starting your new life and everything. I do appreciate you coming. I was just hoping to have a final word with you. One last father, daughter talk before you go." We both paused for a second, so I asked, "Is that ok?"

"That's fine, daddy," she said. "I always have time for you." she walked to the patio and sat down. A natural buzz I was feeling. My nerves were so shot, I felt fuzzy and disoriented. I took another breath as I paced on the patio, "Daddy, stop pacing. You'll worry yourself to death." She sounded like her mother with those words. "Just sit down and take a deep breath. Let's talk. I love our father, daughter moments." She said with the most innocent face I ever saw.

"This won't take long," I stated. "I just want you to know I am so proud of you. I want to thank you personally for being such a wonderful daughter. It has been an honor being your father. It truly has. So many wonderful memories" - I took a deep breath - "So many memories, it's hard to let go." As tears watered my eyes. I took another breath.

"Oh, daddy, you're going to get me all worked up," she said. "I wouldn't trade you for any other father in the world. You're the best daddy. You know that, right?" She asked.

"Thanks!" I replied. "Listen, before you go out into this world, I need you to know something's. I have always kept a good home for you, but I fear, for fear, that I might have sheltered you from some things in this world. I have no doubt you are going to do great, but the world is not always rainbows and unicorns. This world is good, but there is wickedness in this world. Always remember, it is also a good place. Occasionally you must make it good again. The world is what you make it. Trust me, there will come a time in this life when you will be both confronted and tested by wickedness in this world. 'And now my job is done, you're on your own now.' I want you to know I believe in you. I know you can do it. Always remember who you are. Your mother and I, we are always here for you, anytime. And I always will be. Promise me you'll do good in this world."

"I promise," she said. "You can count on me."

I reached into my pocket and pulled out a pocket watch I carried around for years. I held it in my hands and told her, "I want you to have this, so you always remember me." I knew this would become a great memory for her in this life. I wanted her to have it. I wanted her to remember. A father's work is never done, but a dad's job has a due date. One last thing Before you go.

The Heart-Shaped Chest of Tisal

Welcome to the dessert valley town of Tisal. There are only two types of people in Tisal. Those that live there, and those who are lost. The town has survived generations on its own in the dessert. Once a year, a festival called the SGF is celebrated. A few lucky town members get to take the mining minerals to the surface. A chance to see the modern world. The winners are chosen by a contest.

The contest started a couple of generations ago when the climate of the valley changed. The air got dryer, and the ground got hotter. Resources changed. The town had no choice but to turn to the outside world for aid. The town decided to trade once a year. They created a festival and called it the SGF (Supply Gathering Festival). There is an old Native American folk tale of the first year's contest, it's called, *The Heart-Shaped Chest of Tisal.*

On the first day of the first festival, Alex woke from his bed in anticipation. Long had he yearned for Susan's heart. He was a construction worker like his father, and grandfather before him. Alex was in love with Susan. As kids they played together, but social distance grew between the two lovers. Alex came from a construction family, and Susan came from a political family. Alex did not give up on love. He knew the festival was his last chance at winning Susan's heart.

Alex put on his best blue-denim outfit. He had ironed his outfit the night before, and it looked nice-n'-neat for Susan's eyes. He chose his best pair of boots and headed out the door. The festival events had begun. It was announced that Susan would be one of the scavenger setters. Alex was excited. He was the first person to sign up for the scavenger hunt.

The scavenger hunt was about to begin. The setters held up pictures of their hidden treasures. Susan's was a dead bull's skull. Joey, a local hunter, was especially drawn to the image. Each treasure had a theme. The bull's skull was one of wilderness. This meant it would be found in nature. The contestants took their place at the starting line. Alex was in the front row. Susan recognized him and smiled. A warm joyful feeling came over Alex as he stared at Susan. Her jet-black hair blowing in the wind majestically. A dessert bird flew over her head. It was a Hawk. Alex assumed the bird was a sign, telling him to fly like the wind.

The start-up gun fired, and Alex dashed from the starting line like the wind. He headed directly to the path leading to the forest. At the path entrance he encountered Joey. The path entrance had been rigged, only one person could enter before it closed. Alex and Joey stood before each other, both ready to rumble.

Joey shouted, "You know the rules?"

Alex nodded his head. He knew the rules. Wrestling and bumping were allowed, but no actual combat. Combat was forbidden.

Joey picked up a handful of dry dusty sand-dirt and slapped his hands together. The dirt cloud covered his entire body. This would make his body harder to grip. Alex dashed for the path entrance knowing Joey's intentions for wrestling. Alex decided to bump instead. This would counter Joey's hunter-hands grasp. Alex would use his speed. They both ran toward the entrance.

As Joey came within reach of Alex, "You're Mine," He shouted. Joey moved like the wind. A dust cloud followed Joey like a zephyr in the air. Joey reached out to grab him, but Alex cleverly bumped Joey with his shoulder. He knocked Joey off balance. Alex made his way toward the path entrance. Alex was faster, but Joey was stronger. Joey didn't fall completely. Joey grabbed Alex before he could slip his grasp. He swung Alex around and threw him to the ground. As Alex tumbled,

Joey passed through the path entrance first. Joey had beaten Alex. Alex found himself on his knees watching the path entrance close.

The only way Alex could win now was to climb the Red Fish Lake Falls. It's mystic flow of wonders and local memories. A legend of its infamous cave entrance hidden behind the falls on the upper top side. Anyone who dared to climb the falls risked falling into Red Lake's deepest trench. The very den of the legendary red fish. No one had ever actually seen red fish, but Alex had no other choice. It was the only option he had.

Alex started to climb the falls. The falls were pulsing like a symphony. The water flowed like an orchestra of strings. The splashing water against the rocks like percussion. The air itself blowing like wind chimes. Even Alex's hands and feet moving against the rocks, sounded like crackling snare drums. With every move, Alex was careful not to fall. He climbed until he reached the near top. He started to shake, but only a bit. He began to slide his way under the waterfall.

Alex could hear a child's voice in the air. "Don't look down," The child shouted. The child was standing on the rock ledges of the shoreline.

'Oops, I looked down. I should not have done that,' Alex said to himself. He paused, and then he turned his eyes down and around to Red Lake. He could see the child standing on the rocks, looking up at him like he was a rockstar. Alex smiled as he turned back around and continued to climb. *'Still, no sign of the infamous red fish,'* he thought as he looked around the inner falls. It's darkened watery dimmed light had a shadowy greyness. The top of the lake water at the bottom of the falls looked as black as the night sky itself. Like starring into outer space, only below instead of up. Yet still no sign of the legendary red fish. Alex could feel eyes upon him as if something was watching. He felt he was not alone, as he stared down. Everything was so grey and black. Alex closed his eyes.

Embracing the moment, Alex took in the surrounding environment. Listening to the elemental spirit of the under-falls, he remembered Susan standing on the rock shore close to where that kid had shouted. He could hear Susan's voice in the wind saying, '*Come with me.*' The voice was a memory of a day in their youth together. He visually remembered the events of that day in his mind.

Alex saw a vision in his mind. A flashback of the day he followed Susan to a nearby cave. A cave hidden in the wilderness. In the cave was a special room. In that room was a chest, a heart-shaped chest. He remembered her pulling out two paper-cut birds. She opened the chest and placed the birds together in the chest. She said, "Whoever finds this chest will forever hold my heart. On that day, these two birds will become one. Both birds will receive a great reward on the day this is found." She closed the chest and sealed it with a kiss as she buried the chest.

Alex opened his eyes. He was standing high up on the waterfall's ledge. The hawk he had seen fly by Susan's head at the starting line, flew over the falls. It kept diving down from the top, and circling around the area. "That's what she was talking about," he Said. Now he knew what she meant. '*She must have hidden her treasure piece in that spot. Whoever finds the heart-shaped chest, will not only win her heart, but also the rewarding contest prize.*' Alex reached for the last rock limb to climb, and he pulled himself up. "There it is! The cave entrance." The legends were true. It was exactly as described in the stories he had heard.

Alex took one last look down at the inner side of the falls. The greyness seemed brighter now, and the water was flowing perfect. The hawk was still soaring in the afternoon blue sky. Alex had solved the mystery. He entered the cave and walked until he came to a split in the path. He realized the right-way path would lead him to the forest. When he came out of the cave exit, he was in the forest. He found a path in the forest and headed directly to Susan's hidden cave as he remembered. Alex found the hidden cave, and he entered. The walls were presently different, they had been painted. Many children had painted the walls with their young imaginations. It was beautiful. Alex continued until he reached the room he visioned.

He stood in the place he witnessed his vision. He looked to the spot where he had seen Susan bury the chest. The ground had been altered and the dirt was loosened. Someone had been there recently. This was a good sign. Alex quickly dug up the chest from the ground beneath him. Alex found Susan's heart-shaped chest. He pulled the chest from the ground and blew the dirt and dust off the chest. The metals of the chest shined brightly, just as he remembered. He closed his eyes and thought, '*This must be fate*.' Alex opened the chest and looked down.

In the chest were the two paper-cut birds, nicely preserved. One on each side, both facing each other. In the middle of the birds was an engagement ring. Two birds and a wedding ring, placed in perfect alignment. A reflection of each other's affection. Alex shrugged in disappointment, confused he shouted, "Where is the scavenger treasure?"

A voice came from behind Alex. "You remembered," The voice said. It was Susan. She was standing at the doorway smiling.

Alex turned to look at her. "The treasure is not here," he said.

"Which would you rather have, one day on the surface, or a lifetime of love?"

Alex reached down and grabbed the wedding ring. He walked over to Susan and said, "I wouldn't trade your love for any or all the treasure on earth."

"I do," Susan said with a smile. It was like the warmness of hot cocoa on a cold winter evening. Susan placed her hand out. "I do." She repeated. "I always knew it was you."

Alex placed the ring on her finger. '*My treasure*,' He thought to himself as he took Susan by the hands. "And ... my reward," He said as he place the ring on Susan's finger.

Joey walked into the cave room. He was holding the dead bull-headed skull. He shouted, "I found it." He did so with great pride. It was like his trophy. Like a hunter who mounts his catch on the wall. Alex and Susan laughed, but they both honorably congratulated Joey. When Joey saw the wedding ring on Susan's hand, He congratulated Alex and Susan. "You found treasure too," Joey said. "Ok, I go to the surface now." Joey started to leave.

"Hey Joey!" Alex Shouted.

Joey stopped and turned around.

"If you need a hand, let me know," Alex said.

Joey answered, "Will do, good Alex." Before Joey left, he turned back to Alex one more time. "You good warrior, you almost beat me at forest gate." Joey looked at Susan. "He is good man Susan." Then Joey left.

Alex and Susan shared true loves first kiss. When they left the cave, The dessert bird flew by their heads. The hawk landed on a tree branch. Another hawk came down and perched on the same branch. The lonely dessert hawk had found his mate. Alex wrapped his arms around Susan and the Two birds flew off into the endless horizon of the Dessert evening skyline horizon.

Winter Meat: The Legend of Huntero

When Zeus created the first generation of mankind, he created the perfect generation. Throughout the ages of man, he discovered different generations and labeled them gold, silver bronze, and iron. After the generation cycle was complete, Zeus created four seasons to resemble the generations of mankind. Spring, Summer, Fall, and Winter. Three seasons were plentiful for harvest, but one brought cold death upon the earth. Zeus knew this would be troubled times for his beloved humans. Therefore, he decided to descend one of his most trusted Gods of Olympus, Huntero (Hunt-Tore-oh), to prepare and assist humans for the cold dead winter season. Their survival would be dependent on Huntero's guidance.

Zeus called Huntero to Olympus and explained his mission. Huntero agreed and was proud to assist, but before he descended onto the earth realm surface, Zeus told Huntero, "They'll worship you as a God of Olympus. Make sure you do not place yourself above me, before them." Then, Zeus granted permission unto Huntero, and he was honored to accept. Huntero descended upon the earth realm surface and approached the human city, Citya (Sit-Tie-Yah).

Prince Manki (Man-Key) Spotted Huntero nearing the city gates from his observation patio. The Prince stormed out of the castle gates; only a couple trusted guards accompanied him. Like the wind, he dashed through the city, to the gate as Huntero was approaching. When Huntero came to the gate, Prince Manki embraced him immediately. "Citya most welcomes you, heavenly one," Prince Manki said. He recognized Huntero's angelical presence at first glance. He humbled himself before this stranger at the city gate. "I am Prince Manki. If I may ask, what is your name, sir?"

"Huntero," the stranger at the gate said.

Prince Manki made Huntero feel most welcome. "I will take you to see my father the King. If you will, follow me?" Prince Maki said as he offered his personal guidance to Huntero.

Huntero proudly accepted. Embracing each other's company, they both walked together all the way to the castle. Huntero was very impressed with Prince Manki. He could see why Zeus embraced humans with every beat of his very heartbeat. When they reached the castle, Prince Manki wasted no time. He took Huntero directly to the Throne room of King Dadeo (Dad-E-Oh).

When the King looked unto Huntero; he set aside all business and affairs. He gave Huntero his full undivided attention. "Bless all Olympus! And to what do I owe this pleasure?" King Dadeo shouted, with a Kingly voice.

Huntero stepped forward to the very center of the throne room. "I bring forth the will of Olympus. Mighty Zeus himself, has descended me upon the earth realm surface to assist you for the coming season. If you follow my lead and instructions, you shall survive the coming season," Huntero announced.

The King took note of Huntero's words. "What is this season, you speak?" The King asked.

"Winter!" Huntero shouted, as he moved around the center of the throne room, addressing the entire council. Then he spake, "The winter shall bring forth such harsh cold that leaves on trees shall wither, die, and fall to the ground dead. Your fields will grow no crops. Dirt shall freeze hard as rock, and your forest shall bare naked. Rain shall turn to ice, and snow shall be your land. The vary air itself shall be so cold, layers of clothes you'll need to subdue the freeze. The only warmth you'll find is by your fireplaces', and under your blanket bed sheets."

The council grew fearsome. "Fire," They shouted, as they rent their clothes. Fire was known only as destruction that left ruins in ash. Confused they did not understand. '*How fire could even exist in such conditions*,' they wondered to themselves. The room was in shambles; the council did not know what to think.

Huntero understood, he knew of their fear of fire. "Be not troubled, for even I Huntero was once too. I once shared your concern of fire as well. Know this, the fire I speak of you shall control."

"Who can control fire?" a council member shouted.

"Allow me the honor to show you, and I shall," Huntero stated. "You will use fire for warmth, and to cook your winter meat. Good meat should not be eaten raw. The winter meat shall be your harvest this season, and this one season only. Now and from this day on. But worry not, I will teach you how to hunt. What part of flesh to eat, and what parts not to eat. Also, I will teach you all my ways so that you shall never be without meat in winter seasons to come."

"Winter meat?" The king asked nervously.

"Winter meat," Huntero shouted back firmly. "Your winter harvest shall be like no other season's harvest. Know, that Zeus himself has blessed you with this winter harvest. Olympus has sent me to teach you, my ways. I am Huntero, God of the hunt."

Prince Manki was very interested in this new winter harvest. "How shall we harvest this winter meat?" He asked.

King Dadeo interrupted, "Let us not get ahead of ourselves, Manki." The King fell unto sadness in his heart. He feared this news. He asked Huntero, "What hast thou done to deserve such a harsh season. Has Thou displeased Zeus?"

"Think no such thing, good King. Mighty Zeus has blessed you abundantly." Huntero said. "I'm surest that thou are familiar with the legendary stories of the ages of man. The first generation; the gold age. Was the purest of mankind. Zeus has made the summer season in their honor. The next generation was the silver age. They fell from the golden age's grace. Zeus has created the fall season in their honor. The third generation was the bronze age. Cruel, hateful, evil, and death was their generation. Zeus has created the winter in their remembrance. Then came the Iron age. The fourth generation, who brought honor back to mankind. They sprang the fountain of grace out of darkness. The spring season was created in their honor. When the cycle was complete, Zeus wrapped the generations of mankind into four seasons in a continuous cycle. For this, you should be grateful. You have three seasons of blessing, and only one season of wroth. This is the fate of man, forever. Sealed by the generations of creation."

Relief filled the king's heart. "Citya shall accept your assistance." The king looked unto the entire counsel within his throne room, even unto all the guards. "We shall follow Huntero's guidance this season. Let us be grateful." The room cheered in delight. The King had made a wise decision to accept Huntero.

"You speak wise, King Dadeo," Huntero Shouted with great honor. He was very pleased with the Kings response.

"Now may I inquire, as to, what is winter meat?" Prince Manki asked.

Huntero, once again instructed the council. "Winter meat is not grown; it can only be hunted. It is the meat of the flesh. Winter meat shall become a blessed sacrifice unto you. The living can only survive on consumption. When the land does not produce, life is forced to consume itself, unfortunately. This is in memory of the bronze age generation, the most brutal of generations. It was a kill or be killed generation. But, if you follow my rules, your curse, shall be a blessing onto you. My rules are simple, but they have meaning." Huntero sat down amongst the council, then he explained his rules. "First rule: only hunt in the hunting season, and no other season. Rule two: only take what you need to survive, and nothing more. Rule three: limit your hunger, and never kill an entire animal species. Always leave enough for the animals to reproduce. Do this, and you shall never go without.

Preservation is essential. Rule four: my last and final rule. Honor the code. Always give more than you take. You will learn to tend to nature, and to appreciate your nature. Treat nature rightfully, and nature shall treat you in return the fruits of your labor."

The council was impressed with Huntero's presentation. This hunt was nothing heard in the ears of these men ever before. The council all agreed, the season Huntero spoke of would need great teaching and learning. The words Huntero spoke sounded of abundance descended from very tip of Mount Olympus itself. The assembly began to take an understanding to Huntero's great wisdom. They agreed to learn his ways. Follow his rules and trust his judgements. And so, they did.

The cold winter season came, and the leaves of trees withered to the ground. Fields grew no harvest, and the dirt froze cold as rock. Rain turned to ice, and snow was the land. Even the tops of great lakes had turned to ice. The forest bore naked, and the citizens of Citya only found warmth in layers of clothes by their fireplaces. They learned how to control fire by the teachings of Huntero. They learned to cook by fire and cooked the meat they gathered from hunts. They learned to preserve food and only hunted what they needed to survive. Together, they all survived the winter season and gave thanks and praise to Zeus of Olympus, for sending the great Huntero, God of the Hunt.

When the winter season came to end, they all gathered in celebration. In the very heart of the city of Citya; they all celebrated. When the celebration concluded, they unveiled a great monumental statue. A winter looking wooden figurine of Huntero, their God of the Hunt. Huntero was overwhelmed by their most impressive gestor. He was pleased and felt great honor. He instructed the citizens of Citya not worship him over Zeus. For Zeus himself, had personally forbidden it. Huntero was a servant to Zeus and Olympus, and a Guide to Humans. "Under Zeus, never over," He commanded, and they all agreed. Then, Huntero gathered his belongings. They all said Their farewells as Huntero prepared to leave. Before Huntero left Citya, he raised his glass in front of his statue. A toast of honor to the humans he now embraced. With his final words, he spake, "From this day on, by this statue, I shall call you, my hunters. You have served well." They all toasted together in honor.

Huntero left the city. Outside of the gate from which he came, he walked off into the wilderness. There, he disappeared into the horizon where no human eye could see him ascend back to Olympus. When Huntero ascended back to Olympus, a great comet lit up the sunset skyline. The humans raised their glasses and chanted, "To Huntero, God of the hunt, And to Almighty Zeus, King of Olympus."

The Milked Man

There was blackness and nothing existed. The music in the background faded to complete silence. Humming vibrations slowly crept into existence. A light shined from above, and land appeared below. A sea of water reflected the sunlight in the near distance. A forest of trees could be seen in the skyline landscape horizon. A breeze of wind came upon Miko, and he found himself awakening in a new world. A world created by own subconscious mind. Conscience in a subconscious creation. *'It's beautiful,'* Miko thought to himself.

A spirit came upon Miko in his new dreamworld. The spirit offered its assistance. The first offering was a milk factory to be built in the fields. Miko thought milk would be good, and he was thirsty. Miko agreed, and the spirit manifested a great milk factory. The spirit put cows in the pastor, and even put workers in the factory. One of the workers brought Miko his first glass of delicious milk. It was made fresh and tasted like the best glass of milk he ever consumed. Miko drank milk until his thirst was fully quenched. Miko started to get hungry. So, the spirit asked Miko his favorite food preference. Miko suggested sandwiches and the spirit made various animals, and planted wheat in fields. The cows wondered over to the fields and began to eat the wheat prematurely. Miko panicked, but the spirit said not to worry. The spirit created farmers to mend fences and keep the cows to their plain. The farmers planted seeds to feed the cows and tended to the various animals. They made Miko sandwiches and gave him milk to drink. Miko ate and drank till he was full.

Miko got tired and wanted to rest. The spirit provided carpenters to build Miko a home to rest. Miko rested in his new home. Before he fell asleep, the spirit asked if he could keep creating while Miko rested. Miko gave consent and permitted the spirit to create. When he woke, the spirit had created an entire city. Miko was impressed with the spirits creations. He went into the city and looked at all the beautiful works the spirit had created. There was restaurants to eat, and shops full of goodies. Miko looked at a shoe store full of shoes. He stated that he could not possibly wear all the shoes displayed. The spirit replied that the workers would wear the shoes he did not need, and that everyone could enjoy the materials provided. He showed Miko how one team of workers fed another team of workers. How all their works would circle around for each other's needs. Miko was most pleased, and the spirit told him that he liked to create. Miko was not displeased in anyway, but he began to wonder what his purpose was. Miko went for a self-walk by the sea, and while he stood on the shoreline, he wondered what he could make in his new world. Inspired by all the spirit's manifestations, he began wanting to create as well. Miko had never built anything before. Miko walked back to the city to find the friendly spirit.

The spirit was in a skyscraper, in the middle of the city. Miko entered the building and a service man in uniform stood at a desk in front of the elevator. Miko told the service man that he was there to see the spirit, but the service man refused to let him pass. He said the spirit was resting. Miko thought the spirit did not rest, but the spirit did rest.

Miko left the building and wondered the streets. The shops were open, but the other places were forbidden. He was not allowed in the offices or the factories. The neighborhoods were for residents only.

Miko looked around the city for tools and materials to build. He eventually found tools to build, and materials to use. The workers were glad to assist. Then he realized, there was no room to build. The land was completely filled with all of the spirits creations. The spirit had built so much, even Miko's house property was downsized. He went searching for more land, but could not find any land, anywhere. Miko felt trapped. The spirit came upon Miko near the forest. Miko asked if there was any way to create more land, but the spirit said it was not possible. The spirit questioned why Miko wanted to go into the forest. Miko told the spirit he needed space to build. The spirit was confused and wondered why Miko wanted to build. '*Silly*,' the spirit thought. The spirit had created everything Miko could possibly need. The spirit's creations were ubiquitous throughout the land, but Miko stated it was not everything he needed.

"This is my land," Miko said. "But I am locked out of most of it by your creations."

"Do these creations, not serve you?" The spirit asked.

"Do they? Or do they serve you?" Miko asked.

The spirit answered, "Maybe they serve both of us."

"I wish that were so," Miko stated.

"How so is that?" The spirit asked.

"What good is all this land, if there is none left for me?" Miko said.

"How can I help, Miko?" The spirit asked.

"I think you've helped enough, spirit. Leave me to my thoughts. Maybe, I am overreacting, then again... maybe not. I need to think. I forbid you to create anything new until I figure this out," Miko said to the spirit.

The spirit headed back to his skyscraper tower and waited for Miko. He did not create anything new. He just waited for Miko innocently in his tower. Miko went back to his house and rested his head. Miko fell asleep. Blackness came over everything and nothing existed. The humming faded and so did its vibration. Music began to creep in the background. A familiar song was playing. It was getting louder. Miko squinted his eyes, and then he opened them. When Miko awoke, he was back in the real world. He awoke in his bed and remembered every bit of the dream he had. He decided to go see his counselor friend for advice.

Miko told the Counselor his dream. After he finished, the professor in curiosity asked, "What was the first thing the spirit built?"

"A milk factory," Miko answered.

"Well, then the answer is obvious."

"What's that?" Miko asked.

The Counselor replied, "Miko, your too nice."

"What does that mean?" Miko asked.

"Your dream is telling you to be careful who you trust."

"Do you think, my dream is warning me?" Miko asked.

"You dream is your subconscious communicating with you. Your higher self is telling you something. Only you can figure out what that truly is," the Counselor stated. "But one thing is obviously apparent."

"What?" Miko asked.

The Counselor replied, "Miko my friend... I hate to say this, but you got milked, man."

The Black Screen

Let me tell you a story about a time not too long ago, when I was almost late for the first time in my life. I have dedicated my life and my reputation to always be on time. I am a person who is always on time. For this, I am respected by numerous pillars of the community. My reputation exceeds me. When I was young a very special person came into my life. This person was a psychic with special abilities. This very spiritual enlightened person told me never to be late. They said, If I was ever late (even once), my entire reality would shift. This effect would change my timeline, and my life forever. I decided, I would never be late. Years passed and my reputation grew. I became a reliable person (a person people could depend on). Never, not once, have I ever been late to anything. One day it almost happened.

It was a Tuesday afternoon when I finished my final report for a major client. The power went out in the whole city. My report was finished, but with no power I was unable to email the report to my client. So, I decided to deliver the report myself in-person. I knew that if I hurried, I could make it there before 5pm closing time. I ran to the nearest subway station to catch the train. When I arrived at the station, I realized the next train would be a bad choice. I might save time sitting in the station, but the route had too many stops. The first train would take forever to reach my destination. I knew the second train with less stops was a faster route to my destination. Both trains would be cutting it close, but I decided to take the second train.

I pulled out my phone while I waited for the train, but my phone was dead. The battery was drained, and my phone had no power. The face screen on my phone was completely blacked out. It was the black screen of death. I thought to myself, '*Oh no, this can't be good.*' My phone was the secret to my success, and I felt naked without it. '*How will I make it in time?*' I wondered as I frantically scrambled my thoughts. I did not see the second train coming into the station. If it wasn't for that boarding bell, I would have missed the train entirely. When I heard the bell, I noticed the train and dashed in a hurry to the nearest available train car. I accidently chose the most crowded train-car on the whole train. I found myself standing in a jam-packed train car with barely enough room to even breathe. Everyone was bumping into each other with every sway. If music had been playing, we would have looked like a swaying symphony, moving in sync to an orchestral rhythm.

On the train, there was a large-sized man. He was blocking the train door every time it opened. At every stop people were pushing and shoving to get off the train, but the large man resentfully stood his ground proudly. Finally, my destination was the next stop. I started to move toward the train's exit door early; I wanted to get a good head start. People began looking at me displeased as I nudged my way toward the train exit door. I whispered to them softly that the upcoming exit was my stop. They understood and told me to go ahead, but the large man would not budge for anybody. As the train reached the station, the large man passed gas, and dis so very loudly. The force of the crowd escaping his disgusting windy smell was like a game of tug and war. Unfortunately, I had no choice. I noticed a child laughing hysterically. He shot two thumbs up to the large gentleman. Silently telling him, "Good One." The man thumbed back to the child. "Right on kid," he silently said back as they exchanged smiles and winks.

I had two choices. Either overcome the stench of the large man's gas bomb and get off the train or accept the fact my whole world might change forever. I decided to go-for-it and get off that train as fast as possible. I took a deep breath while the air was still fresh, and I held my breath for as long as I could hold. '*Can I make off this train in time?*' I asked myself. When the train doors opened, the crowd scattered for fresh air. I made a hundred-yard dash sprint for the door. "I made it," I shouted out loud as I stepped off the train. A sense of relief came over me.

After I got off the train, I pulled out my phone to check the time, but the screen was still black. The black screen of death was upon me. I looked around for a clock, but they had all been removed. No one uses clocks anymore. Once where payphones, newsstands, and clocks used to be, were now just painted walls. Not even a map was on the wall. I found myself standing in the middle of a no information station. I was absolutely stunned at the realization of progressive world changes. I left the station, and I walked the city streets. I began to wonder if I smelled. Realizing I previously ran through an odor. I was sniffing myself, as I surged the city streets. I asked a couple of strangers if I smelled alright. They said that I smelled decent, but maybe they were just being nice. Maybe they don't care. I looked around for sweet scents, but I couldn't find any. Finally, I gave up looking.

'*What time is it?*' I kept asking myself as I frantically paced the city streets. At the corner street crossing there was a man peddling a bicycle taxi. He looked at me and asked, "Do you need a ride?" I looked at my phone, but the black screen of death was still upon me. "Aw man! That really sucks," he said. I asked the man how long it would take to reach my destination. He said it would take less than two minutes to get there. "Hop On! I'll get you there," He shouted. He pulled out a can of spray and sprayed the seat. Rosemary banana was the scent, and it smelled beautiful. '*This was my guy,*' I thought to myself as I jumped into his passenger carriage. '*My knight in shining armor had arrived in his embassy of sweet-smelling delightfulness.*'

When we arrived, I ran into the office building. I ran up the stairs and into my client's office. My client was super excited. He was very pleased that my report (he so eagerly waited on) had arrived. "Man, do you ever let anyone down?" he asked.

I replied with a proud, "no... never!" We shook hands and closed the deal. I was so happy my reality was saved; I had made it on time. I looked down at my phone and the black screen of death was still there. I asked my client, "Do you mind if I charge my phone?"

My client looked back at me and replied, "I would love to help you, but the power is out."

A Box of Secrets

In the shiny-polished interior office of the towering 64-story skyscraper, cooperate CEO, Mr. Winslough, came up with a delightful devious plot. He decided to test-prank his GM (General Manager) named Derek. He took an empty box off his shelf and closed it tight, making sure it would close but not lock. Only he, himself, knew the box was completely empty.

Mr. Winslough stepped into the elevator and traveled two-floors down. He entered Derek's office and said, "Guard this box." He told Derek the box had company secrets. Secrets that could be consequential and career-changing for the company and employees. That's all he said, and then he left. Mr. Winslough went back to his fancy office at the top of the building. He then watched the security camera monitors closely, watching every movement with an itch of anticipation.

At first, Derek was excited. Feeling trusted, he was proud to hold the box. Soon his curiosity began to wonder what was inside. He inspected the box. *'It's not locked,'* he thought to himself. The temptation grew unbearable, and Derek could no longer resist. So, he gave the box to Lisa, his secretary. He instructed her not to peep inside.

Lisa placed the box on her desk and went back to her duties, typing as if the box were not even there. When she finished typing, the box strangely attracted her. She had never seen such a box before. It was black lathered, and nicely polished. *'Whoever's box this is, it's well crafted.'* she thought. *'It obviously must have something important inside.'* She could not take her attention off the box; she was mesmerized by its beauty. The leather was soft and moist: not dry or rough. She swayed her fingers across the box with stokes of Pleasure.

Kathy from down the hall walked into the office and asked Lisa if she could help. Lisa always helps Kathy, but she knew she had to watch the box. Confused she wondered, '*What shall ever, shall I do?* The clock stroked 11:11(AM) and Joey, the janitor, walked in. Lisa shouted, "Oh! Thank heaven." She asked Joey if he would watch the box while she helped Kathy. Joey was happy to oblige. Lisa knew she could trust Joey, but before she left, she told him, "No snooping." Lisa left the office to assist Kathy.

Joey started cleaning the office. He had to move the box to clean the desk. He could smell the polish cleaner used on the box. Likewise, he loved that smell. When he picked up the box, he thought to himself, '*It's so light.*' Something oddly peculiar was calling his attention to the fresh scented box. "What the heck is in this box?" He said out loud. An unexpected puzzling mystified his thoughts as he started to believe the box was empty. '*Is this a joke?*' He wondered. He began to laugh. "Oh! These office people are always playing silly jokes," he said as he put the box down on the ground and began cleaning the desk. He went about his business, cleaning the rest of Lisa's workspace.

Derek Marched swiftly out of his office and asked joey, "Where is Lisa?"

Joey answered, "She went to help Kathy."

Derek grabbed the box broadly and took it back into his office. He couldn't take the temptation anymore; he had to know. He opened the box and to his surprise, the box was completely empty. Stunningly confused, Derek began to question Mr. Winslough, '*Is Mr. Winslough out of his mind? Is the old man losing it?*' All he could ask himself was, '*Why did Mr. Winslough give me an empty box, and why did he say it was secret?*'

Lisa came on the intercom saying, "Mr. Winslough on line one."

"Derek!" Mr. Winslough's voice shouted over the intercom. "Please come up to my office. Oh! And bring the box with you."

Derek answered immediately, "Yes sir, I'm on my way." Derek closed the box and headed for the elevator. In the elevator, Derek was sweating, nervous, shaken-up, and confused. Holding an empty box, wishing he had not known its true secret of emptiness. When The elevator door opened, Derek went into Mr. Winslough's office. He handed him the box.

Mr. Winslough examined every inch of the box. Taunting Derek with every inspection. Then he asked, "Did you open this?"

Derek paused. "I thought you trusted me," he stated.

Mr. Winslough laughed. He laughed so hard he had to sit down with his belly full of jiggles. "Trust you?" He shouted in a loud authorities tone. Then, he calmly said, "Well I do now. Now that I know, you opened this box." He eyeballed Derek face to face. "Don't deny it, I saw you on camera."

Derek broadened his shoulders and stood abundantly straight. "Now, Mr. Winslough," he said, but Mr. Winslough Interrupted him.

"Stop right there, Derek. Let's not take this too far. I know you're a loyal man. I know exactly why you looked inside. You wanted to know what was so important. Those secrets! I like that integrity in a man. Get those facts, do what needs to be done. We need that kind of spunk-fire around here. Derek, I am officially promoting you to my personal understudy. That is, if you'll accept."

"Yes sir, Mr. Winslough. Thank you!" Derek answered.

As Derek walked out of the office the old man was laughing hysterically. Derek stepped into the elevator and thought to himself, *'If this is a promotion, I'd hate to see what an actual firing looks like.'* Nothing like a box of secrets to liven' the place up.

The Kool-Aide

As a man... Marcus Thompson never cried, pushed his father, yelled at his mother, disowned friends, feared his community, hid from the police, ran from a doctor, or told a preacher to burn in hell. Life has ways of testing us, and with life, you never know what's coming next, but imagine if you will. What if I showed you someone pouring poison into a drink, would you drink it? Could anyone convince you otherwise? Would anybody believe you if you told them? How many people do you think would attempt to persuade, force, or deceive you into drinking the poison, and even more so... Who? Anyone who tries to subdue you to drink the Kool-aide, is not your friend. With every attempt, your enemies will reveal themselves to you. No matter how hard they try to disguise themselves, imagine if you knew the truth.

Marcus Thompson woke in his bed after having the strangest dream. Marcus dreamt of grayness that clouded the air, and all he could see outside the broken, stained window was the carcasses of dead bodies piled one upon another. There, on a freshly polished redwood table in his bedroom, was a Collins glass filled halfway with a reddish-blackened liquid, and a message written on the wall with blood. '*Don't drink the Kool-Aide.*'

Marcus went downstairs for breakfast. His mother served him scrambled eggs, bacon, and toast, Marcus' favorite. As he took that first delicious bite of crispy bacon, his mother placed a drink on the table. It was a Collins glass filled halfway with a reddish-blackened liquid; The very drink he had dreamt. "No Kool-aide for me today, Mom." He told his mother.

Marcus' father walked into the kitchen and sat down. "We don't waste in this house," he said. Marcus noticed both his mother and father were acting strange. They were fixated on that drink. They couldn't take their hidden third eyes away from it, and Marcus was getting some creepy vibes. Marcus' father picked up the glass and placed it in the refrigerator. "Maybe later," he said.

As Marcus ate, his mother pulled the Kool-Aide out of the refrigerator and placed it back on the table. "Drink up," she said (so-ever-so sweetly), but Marcus refused to take even one sip. His resistance was getting harder to manage. Mom got upset. "What's wrong with you?" She asked as she stood hoovering over him staring at the Collins glass.

Saved by the bell... or doorbell that is. The doorbell rang and Marcus lunged eagerly to answer the door. It was Amelia; he hadn't seen her company in years. 'Why is Amelia here,' He thought.

"We've got to go... Now!" Amelia frantically shouted. "Wait! You didn't drink the Kool-Aide did you?" She asked.

Marcus shook his head, No!

Amelia stated she had witnessed Doctor Edmund pouring poison into the Kool-Aid. He was trying to poison the whole town. Unfortunately, it was already too late for most people.

"What happens if you drink the Kool-Aid?" Marcus asked

"Come with me, and I'll show you," Amelia said. She grabbed Marcus' arm, and they ran toward the town of O'Bestel—an old English town known for its historic 1940s prosperity. Today, most people in town are modern-day people, but the place still looks historic. Some people still dress in 1940s attire to entertain visiting tourists. When they reached town, Amelia instructed Marcus not to be seen or discovered. Together, they snuck around O'Bestel unseen. When they reached Main Street, Amelia told Marcus that anyone who drinks Dr. Edmund's poisoned Kool-Aide will either die suddenly or become unconsciously enslaved (under hypnosis caused by the drink). The town's people were all standing in the park under a trance.

When Marcus witnessed the town's people he uttered, "That rotten, no-good, two-timing snake. I should make him drink his own Kool-Aid. That would teach him a lesson."

Amelia gave Marcus the stare, like when they were young. She would always correct him. "I don't think he would drink his own poison. He knows what it does," Amelia stated.

"Exactly! That's a fantastic idea, Amelia. Wait here; I'll be right back."

Marcus left Amelia's side and cleverly crept into the Main Street restaurant, where Chef was preparing Dr. Edmund's lunch (A juicy twelve-ounce sirloin steak with baked potato). Marcus slithered in quietly through the backdoor unnoticed. When he reached the kitchen, he spotted a barrel of Kool-Aide sitting on top of the ice tray. The waitress poured a glass of Kool-Aide and assisted Chef in serving a big order. The kitchen was clear. Marcus dashed to the drink station and found a Collins glass. He filled the glass halfway with Kool-Aide, just like the other glasses.

"What are you doing in here?" Chef shouted as he entered the kitchen and found Marcus.

"Can you keep a secret?" "Dr. Edmund accidentally drank the wrong drink. He thinks he took his Kool-Aide, but it was the wrong glass. I am trying to figure out a way to give him his Kool-Aide, without alerting him to his error. Then, he would have his medicine, and wouldn't know he made such a clumsy mistake."

"That's easy!" Chef said. "Give it here, and hand me my syringe."

Marcus handed Chef the Collins glass and reached for the syringe. "Are you sure this will work?" Marcus asked Chef.

"I do this all the time," Chef stated as he loaded the syringe. "This syringe is how I inject savory flavors into my steaks." Chef began to inject the Kool-Aide into the steak. "I will load the steak with

Kool-Aide. The Doc will never know." Chef reached up and grabbed a spice bottle. He began to spice up the steak. "Lemon, pepper, garlic... The Doc's favorite. He won't taste a thing," Chef said. Marcus thanked Chef and they both promised to keep it a secret.

Marcus left the restaurant and crept back to Amelia. He told her what he did, and they both laughed as Dr. Edmund entered the restaurant. They watched with anticipation as Dr. Edmund ate his steak. Unfortunately for the Doc, he was not immune to the Kool-Aide. With his last bite, he corked over and died on the floor instantly. As the Town's people circled around the restaurant commotion, Marcus painted a message on the town wall for everyone to see. The message read, *Don't drink the Kool-Aide.*

Kennel Club

On a cloudy dim-lit day, Joseph received a call he will never forget. A call that changed his life forever. He received news that his beloved grandfather had passed away. His grandfather left him the family business property. A racetrack called, *The Kennel Club*. Joseph agreed to accept the racetrack known for many infamous greyhound dog races. The track was a local historical location. Joseph knew he was not his grandfather. Joseph was proud and honored to step-up and take ownership.

Joseph arrived at the Kennel Club. Much to his desire, the place was a dump, ran-down and falling apart. The bleachers stood empty and closed for years due to safety regulations. Only the concession stand, standing viewing area, and VIP clubhouse section were open. Everything else, closed. The entire stadium was out of commission.

Joseph decided to fix the place up. So, he decided to visit some local banks and see if there was anything he could do. He found two local bankers whose yearly annual loan quotas needed met. These two bankers took a personal special liking to the idea of a racetrack. If Joseph paid off the loan it would be a profit, but if he fell short, the bank would own a racetrack. It was gamble from the very beginning. Joseph and the two bankers agreed to terms. Joseph would have one race season to pay off the loan. Only one season. Joseph accepted the loan and began the renovations.

Melissa, a girl who graduated high school, decided to spend her last summer with her father who was a dog trainer. One last summer before college. Melissa's father decided it was time for Rocket to race professionally. Rocket, a young perfectly bred greyhound race dog that Melissa had raised since a pup. Rocket was Melissa's favorite greyhound. They took Rocket to the Kennel Club and began his training.

Growing up in the world of racing, Joseph had seen dogs come and go all his life. He could spot a winner at first glance. When Joseph saw Rocket training on the track, he knew Rocket was a winner. As he watched Rocket run, he thought, '*Wow, that dog is the fastest dog have ever seen.*'

Joseph looked at his grandfather's statue near the opening entrance. The statue had a quote engraved into a brass plate that read, '*ROOT! ROOT! For the home team.*' Joseph's grandfather used to always say this quote, all the time. It was, after all, the secret to his grandfather's success. Joseph's grandfather made his fortune at a local track upstate. He spotted a local dog with potential. No matter where his grandfather went, he always rooted for the home team, or betted on a local champion. Joseph's grandfather bet the farm on a local talent, and it paid off. He was so excited, he built his own racetrack , and that's how the Kennel Club was born.

As Joseph stared at the quote engraved on his grandfather's statue, he thought to himself, 'Bet it all on Rocket.' He stood up and shouted, "Root! Root! For the home team." A couple locals shouted back. They laughed and thought it was joke, but they had no clue what Joseph had discovered. Joseph sat down and decided to end the summer race season with a special event. He looked at his loads. He had enough. It would be a long shot, a really long, long shot, but he had enough.

Joseph created an international championship race at his new up-to-date renovated racetrack. The international Kentucky Derby of greyhound dog racing. With his new up-to-date website app, and the new laws in place, It was actually possible to pull this event off. The International Finals, he called the event. Eight dogs from eight countries will compete in one race for the cup. He could stream the race on the app and take international bets from all over the world. *'One big payday,'* He thought to himself as he stood up and dashed to his office. In his office, he made all the preparations.

The summer started, and the track stadium restored to its former glory. The racing season begun, and all the legends of guest and sports fans came to see the new renovated track. He had music artist and bands perform. The stands were now full of everyday people enjoying the races. The concession stands had good food and clean kitchens. Everybody loved the track. Even the online app was successful. Bets were coming from everywhere. Then, in the very last race at the grand re-opening ceremony, Rocket made his first appearance debut.

Many spectators where skeptic of betting on a new dog they had never seen run. Joseph got excited when he saw Melissa and her father walked Rocket to the start gate. Melissa gave Rocket a big hug and a kiss. She whispered in Rocket ear, "Do his best." When they closed the start-up cage, Rocket stood firm, quite as a dog could be. His eyes focused on the runway racetrack.

Out of the box came Fluffy, the mechanical bunny. Rocket gripped his feet in the starting cage, getting a good sturdy starting position. Rocket's eyes followed Fluffy as he approached. When the cage doors opened, Rocket was the first dog out of the start-up cage. The crowd could not believe their eyes, Rocket was so fast. All the other dogs were eons behind him, as he charges out the gate. The crowd cheered as Rocket led the entire race and placed first.

"Root! Root! For the home team," Joseph shouted.

All season long, Rocket kept winning. 1st place every time. His stat sheet made him the best in the USA. Rocket qualified for the international finals championship event. The bankers began to worry for Joseph. Rocket was winning so big; everyone was betting on him and winning big. The payouts were shifting. The bankers wondered if Joseph was going to be able to pay off the loan." Joseph paid it no mind;

he had a plan. He told the bankers he had every bit of confidence that he make the payment. The bankers took Joseph at his word.

At the end of the summer race season, the international finals came. Ten races, with many dogs from all over the world ran the opening races. All the dogs were Top competitors, and the wage bets were all over the playing field. Guest experienced some of the best greyhounds around the world. One big event, and for the first time in their lives. It was exciting. The online app with the live stream, was jam packed. Millions of viewers from all over the world were watching.

Melissa and her father knew this was their last night together before Mel goes off to college. They spend some good quality time together before the final race. When they announced the final race, Melissa and her father got Rocket ready. This was the main event. This is what everyone came to see.

The final race line-up was Bucky (France), Yusuf (India), Georgie (UK), Judah (Middle East), Noszka (Russia), Tucky (Ireland), Lepas (Australia), and Rocket (USA). All the dogs were showcased center stage and walked to the startup gate.

Everyone was nervous, even Joseph, and especially the bankers. The office was on the fritz. Everything was riding on this race. Sink or swim, this was it. The final moment had come. The crowd roared as they closed the startup gate. Rocket was the tamest dog in the cage. Rocket had never gone up against other top bred dogs. This was a challenge. *'Can he do it?'* melissa asked herself, as she worried over Rocket. Her favorite greyhound in the whole world, that she raised from a pup.

A loud bell rang throughout the stadium. Fluffy the mechanical bunny came rushing out of his mechanical box. The crowd cheered; all bets were final. Rocket's eyes fixed on Fluffy, the bunny was moving faster than ever before. The technicians wanted to make sure that Fluffy did not got caught or become some dogs chew toy. These were, after all, the fastest greyhounds in the world. All in one race.

"Root! Root! For the home team," Joseph shouted from the owner's box at the top of VIP clubhouse section.

"Root! Root! For the home team," Everyone in the VIP clubhouse section shouted.

Fluffy stormed around the starting line and the startup cage gates opened. All the dogs charged out of the cage. Head-to-head, fighting for every inch. Rocket kept up at good pace. He was the youngest greyhound in the race pack. The greyhounds were side-by-side. Equal in position, not one behind; not one ahead. On the first turn, Rocket took the lead and the crowd cheered. On the second turn, Georgie and Noszka passed Rocket. Rocket was now in third place. The crowd panicked, most of them had bet the farm on Rocket.

The bankers secretly smiled. '*Maybe this will pay off*,' they thought. Joseph was as calm as the breeze that day. He sat back and enjoyed the race as Rocket, Noszka, and Georgie ran the back stretch straight way. Rocket caught up. It was a three-way tie; A fight for first place. The crowd cheered.

Joseph clapped his hands, and shouted, "Root! Root! For the home team,"

"Root! Root! For the home team," Everyone in the VIP clubhouse section shouted.

On the third Turn, Rocket took the lead. The crowd roared and the bankers got worried. On the final turn, Lepas Creeped up next to rocket. Bucky slipped into 3rd, passing Noszka. It was Rocket and Lepas tied in first place, coming around the turn. Bucky was 3rd with Noszka in fourth. Yusuf and Judah bumped each other and fell out of the race. Disqualified, which can, and has happened in real greyhound dog racing. Tucky jumped over the dogs falling and was still in the race, now in fifth place. Unfortunately, Bucky was in last place, a lost cause at this point.

The crowd cheered in all the excitement. This was exciting as it gets. Rocket and Lepas dashed for the finish line, Head-to-head. Some people in the crowd could not take all the anticipation. The moment was so intense. Everyone else, watch every inch of that final race. To this day, they still watch the replay, and sometimes in slow motion. This was a moment in Greyhound racing history.

In that moment, Rocket did something he had never done before. He looked at Melissa and her father standing at the finish line. Melissa blew Rocket a kiss, and Rocket smiled. Even the video shows the dog smiled. It was a big smile. Then, Rocket got low to the ground. He pushed himself up with a great force and passed Lepas but a mile. There was no debate; Rocket won the cup.

The crowd roared so loud. Not only did the entire stadium shake, but regulars say, the whole town area shook like a earthquake that day. The stadium roared like a raging Storm.

The bankers lowered their heads. Sure, they loved the race and all the excitement. They felt bad for Joseph. He tried so hard, and it was a good thing he did. They pondered back and forth to themselves, looking to see if they could extend the loan.

Joseph stood up in his owners box and shouted "Root! Root! For the home team."

"Root! Root! For the home team," the entire stadium shouted.

Joseph turned around and headed for his office. When he sat down, the two bankers came into his office.

"It was a good show," One of the bankers said.

"What, are you crazy? That was the greatest show on earth." Joseph said. "And thank my lucky blessings it turned out the way it did. Or you would be the proud new owners of the family built and operated Kennel Club." Joseph signed a check and handed the check to the bankers. His loan payment in full.

The bankers took the check. One of the bankers asked, "But, How?"

"What do you mean?" Joseph asked.

"Everyone bet on Rocket. How can you profit if everyone won?" The banker asked.

"Who said everybody won. Did you forget the app."

"What does that even mean?" The banker asked.

"This was a global event. Everyone betted on their country. Like I said, Thank my lucky blessings India didn't win. Did you know India has a billion citizens. America only has three hundred million. If India had won, I will be in real trouble." Joseph laughed.

The bankers didn't realize all the gamblers had bet on their own countries. Putting the odds 7 to 1 in any one country's favor. Joseph stood up and shook the bankers hands. "Like I said fellas... Root! Root! For the home team."

"Root! Root! For the home team" The bankers shouted.

Before the bankers left, Joseph told them, "It was a gamble from the very beginning, but like my grandfather always said, always bet on the home team... always."

Barry Loves Fried Tuna

Inspecter Joe came to visit Gary's little bodega restaurant in the city. Upon his arrival, he noticed the strangest thing occurring in the kitchen. The chef (Gary) was frying Tuna; or at least, a portion serving size amount. Inspector Joe could not take his eyes away from this strange phenomena.

"Why are you frying the Tuna?" Inspector Joe asked.

"Barry only eats fried Tuna," Gary answered.

"Who eats fried Tuna?"

"Barry," Gary stated.

Gary added one tablespoon of teriyaki sauce, and a pinch of garlic on top of the two scoops of butter sizzling under the frying Tuna. He chopped 2 cups of broccoli and added the greenery to the frying pan. A dash of salt and pepper, and the smell in the kitchen was nothing Joe had ever smelt before. The smell of fried tuna was intriguing but infuriating at the same time. Barry came through the entrance door and sat at his favorite table.

"Coming right up," Gary shouted from the kitchen.

Gary scooped the fried Tuna onto a slice of toasted bread. He placed nothing but tomato and mayo on top. He closed the sandwich and scooped two scoops of coleslaw on the side. He served the dish to Barry personally. Barry grabbed the fried Tuna sandwich and took the most disturbing, unmannered, big bite, Joe had ever witnessed.

"Um-Hum," Barry groaned as he chomped down that Fried Tuna sandwich.

Gary turned to inspector Joe in the kitchen and said,

" I fried.
I served.
He ate."

VOLT: The Power Outage

In the late-night hours of the new day midnight, there was a power outage all over the modern-day western town of Butte, Montana. From the spectacular view of Granite Mountain at Berkeley Pit to the World Museum of Mining, the power was out. The light of the brightly full crested moon somehow gave that old Mining Tower (historic landmark), a luminous glow in the pitch-black darkness of the midnight hours.

Sheriff Haggis was going floor to floor at St. James Hospital to see if everyone was o.k. Luckily, all the patients were stable. He stepped outside the hospital and walked to his squad car to check his police radio. Silent as the night itself; the radio was. He began to drive around town, instructing everyone to contact him on his radio if they needed any assistance. Driving up and down main street, he stopped at a red-light in front of the Hotel Finlen.

A voice came on his radio. "Sheriff," the voice said. "Are you there?"

The Sheriff pulled into the empty parking lot of the Hotel Finlen and answered, "This is Sheriff Haggis, go-head."

"Well, let the party begin," the voice said. "Don't you get too comfortable. You're in for a long night, Sheriff."

"Who is This?" The Sheriff asked.

"Just call me Buddy," the voice said.

"O.k. Buddy, how can I help you?" the Sheriff said in a calm voice as he sipped his coffee.

"No, Sheriff, how can I help you?" buddy said.

Sheriff Haggis paused; he was confused. He had no idea who he was talking too. No clue to what Buddy's intentions were. The two went back-n-forth on the radio for a bit of time. Questions, no sense answers, mind-games, and quotes that made no sense to the Sheriff Haggis. The voice on the radio would only state his name was Buddy, and he was there to help. The whole matter made no sense to the Sheriff, so he decided to investigate the power outage. He restarted his car and went to the power company.

When the Sheriff arrived at the power company, they directed him to the location of the power outage. As he drove to the site, the radio was quiet. Buddy wasn't talking. He pulled up next to where the workers were working. He got out of his car and headed over to speak with the electricians on-site.

"This was no accident," one of the electricians said as he showed the Sheriff the wreckage that caused the power outage. The Sheriff could see, clear-as-day, the entire unit had been sabotaged. The cuts were clean, and circuits had been rewired. The power switch must have been turned off manually before the sabotage took place. Whoever did this, had to be a professional.

The workers said it would take all night to fix the damage. "Power should be back on by sunrise," one of the electricians said. The Sheriff went back to his car to call-it-in and give an update after speaking with the electricians. When the Sheriff got into his car, The voice of Buddy came on his radio.

"Sheriff," Buddy said. "Sheriff, are you there?" He said again.

"This is Sheriff Haggis; Buddy, is that you?" He asked.

"Yeah, it's me. You're not going to believe this Sheriff," Buddy stated. "You need to get back to main street. Call in back-up. Do not go alone. I repeat, do not go alone."

The Sheriff started his engine. He slapped the gear into drive and headed for main street. When he arrived, his eyes could not believe what he was seeing. A massive crowd of Mining activists were organized in protest all over main street. Screaming and yelling up and down the street. They were not completely against minerals or the use of minerals. They were, however, against the mining companies' damaging production practices and their greedy consumption. "Respect the earth," they shouted. "Don't ruin nature," They chanted. The crowd grew Louder and louder with every chant. "Money over miners. Money over mankind," they screamed.

Sheriff Haggis immediately tuned his radio onto a federal channel. "This is Sheriff Haggis," he said. "We got a riot in downtown Butte. I repeat, we got a riot in downtown Butte. Please send back-up immediately. The Power is out, and the streets are filled with protesters. Please send all available emergency units now."

The operator's voice came on the radio. A woman operator replied, "Sheriff, we read you. Ten-four, copy that."

The Sheriff clicked the talk button, "This is not a drill. This is the real thing."

She replied, "Copy that, Sheriff. Units are on their way. E.T.A. forty-five minutes."

"Forty-five minutes! This place will be toast by then," he said out-loud to himself off the radio. He put the radio down and moved his car. He chose an observation location for his local deputies to pull up. Sirens all over town were ringing as the entire force and local responders were on their way.

When they arrived, the Sheriff directed them not to engage the crowd. "Stand down!" The Sheriff shouted at his deputies as they arrived. "Stand down, back-up is on the way," he continued to say.

The crowd ramped rigorously as they began to smash windows, tear down statues, and spray paint downtown. Sheriff Haggis ordered his deputies to pull out cameras or use their phones to take pictures. "Capture as much activity footage as you can," The Sheriff ordered.

The crowd started moving from the downtown area to the Mill Tower (Historical landmark) at the World Museum of Mining, where the local mining facilities were located. The Sheriff was nervous about the residential homes in between the two locations. He had no choice; he ordered all responders to head to the Mountain peak of the mountain with a big sign of the letter 'M' on it. From there, they could overlook the situation.

"Get to 'M' Mountain peak," the Sheriff ordered. When he got into his car, Buddy's voice came on the radio.

"Sheriff, are you there?" Buddy asked.

"Go-head," the Sheriff answered.

"Man, you got your hands full tonight."

"That's a big Ten-four. Tell me something I don't know," the Sheriff stated.

"Oh, there's a lot you don't know, Sheriff."

"Well, if you got something to say; Spit it out. I don't have all night," The Sheriff told buddy.

"Right now, the night is all we have, Sheriff," Buddy replied.

"What's that supposed to mean. Listen, I appreciate your help Buddy, I really do. Unless you have something to tell me, I don't have time for no nonsense right now. I'm busy right now if you couldn't tell," the Sheriff said.

"That's a big ten-four Sheriff," Buddy said. "When you need to know; I'll let you know. You just be ready, Sheriff. Buddy-Out."

The busy, distraught Sheriff put his radio down. He turned onto a paved road that headed to the peak of big 'M' mountain. He parked his car along with all the deputies following him. They all got out of their squad cars, trucks, and department issued vehicles. They gathered at the viewpoint and looked down on all the protesters with a bird's-eye view from above. Twenty minutes had passed. Twenty-five minutes until back-up was to arrive.

The Sheriff did not want to escalate the situation. He told his officers to wait for back-up. The protesters had not damaged the residential area, but now they were coming to the mining facility at the mining museum.

"This is not going to go good," the Sheriff uttered to his deputies standing around him. "Not good at all."

They watched the mob destroy property and vandalize everything they could get their hands on. Climbing the old miner's Mill Tower and tearing pieces off, piece by piece. They broke into the World Museum of Mining; it was a free-for-all. The power was out, and the mob knew it. Deputies stood helpless as the mob devoured the miner's facility.

A deputy coming from the location of the power outage pulled in. "Where's the Sheriff?" He shouted. The deputy walked up to the Sheriff and told him the electricians had good news. The power will be on around sunrise. They were able to fix-it and solve the mess. They also stated that the matter was done by a professional electrician. This information would help the investigation narrow the search to a certified, licensed professional.

The Sheriff thanked the deputy and asked him to return to the power outage site. He instructed the deputy to keep informed of any updates. "Yes, sir," the deputy said. Before the deputy walked away, he asked the sheriff, "How did you get to the protest so fast?"

"Oh, someone came on the radio yapping about it," the Sheriff answered.

"What guy?" He asked rhetorically. "You were there, right as they arrived. I swear," The deputy said. "I don't know who your radio guy is, but there is no way you could have made that timing. That's wild," The deputy said as he walked to his car and drove off.

'That's odd,' the Sheriff thought as the deputy drove away. He turned his focus back to the raging mob of Nature activists. Then he noticed some miners up in the office. He couldn't quite make out who it was. All he could see was a flashlight flickering in the office, and the shadow of a person moving around.

"What's up, Sheriff?" One of the deputies asked.

"Those miners in the office," he answered. 'Must be third shift,' He thought. The Sheriff then headed toward the armor truck. "I need you guys to cover me," he said to the deputies.

"What's the plan, boss?" A deputy asked.

"No plan. I'm going to go get those miners out of there. I need you guys to cover me." He opened the armored truck and began to pull out long-range guns and sniper rifles. He started to hand them out. "I trust you guys; I always have... You guys got me?" The Sheriff asked.

"Yes, sir," all the deputies answered together.

"Alright then. I'm going to head up the back road in that truck. There should be no problem. Get in, get those miners, and get out. If anything goes wrong, you guys know what to do," the Sheriff said.

"We got you," a Deputy said as all the deputies nodded their heads in agreement.

After the Sheriff instructed his deputies, he grabbed his radio and jumped into the armored police issued pick-up truck. As he was starting the truck, Buddy's voice came on the radio. "Buddy, is that you?" The Sheriff asked.

"Yeah, it's me," Buddy said. "How's it going?" Buddy asked.

The Sheriff stopped turning the car key and talked to Buddy. "I would be better if you told me how you knew about that protest. I mean... How you knew, before it happened?" the Sheriff asked with a bit of attitude in his tone.

"Hey, you're waking up. I told you this was going to be a long night," Buddy replied.

"Yes, you did, buddy. So, are you going to tell me?" The Sheriff asked patiently.

"Oh... That! That was easy. They've been organizing this protest for weeks on social media. Man, you guys really are blind. All the information is on their social media page. I thought you guys were all over that stuff," Buddy said, laughing.

"This is a first I'm hearing of it. We're not always up to date on everything. We do our best," the Sheriff said. "Anything else you want to let me in on, Buddy?" He asked.

"You'll know when you need to know, Sheriff. Have faith. All the answers are coming. Trust the process, Sheriff," Buddy said.

"O.k. then... Well... listen. I can't talk right now. I got to go save some miners who need my help right now. I got good people depending on me right now. We'll talk soon," the Sheriff said as he put down the radio.

Buddy's voice came back on the radio, "If You're going up to that office to go get them miners, you better take some back-up, Sheriff."

The sheriff picked the radio back up, "O.k. Buddy. I'm listening." He waited patiently. He then followed, "Tell me what I need to know, I do need to know, don't I?" The Sheriff asked.

"I reckon you do. Things are starting to move faster now, huh? Funny thing about those so-called miners," Buddy stated.

"What's That?" The sheriff asked.

"They haven't had any third shift since the pandemic. I mean, after all those restrictions, this inflation, and not to mention all the cutbacks companies had to make just to make ends-meat. Are you sure them are miners, Sheriff?

"You know what, you're absolutely right, Buddy," the Sheriff replied surprisingly. "I appreciate the heads-up. I didn't even think of that. Must have slipped my mind."

"You got a lot on your plate right now, Sheriff. But hey... You're getting warmer, that's for sure. You be careful up there. Buddy-out.

"Ten-four Buddy. Thanks for the update," the Sheriff said as he put down his radio. He got out of the truck and walked back over to his deputies. As all the deputies gathered around, he shouted, "Change of plans." He informed them of the update he just learned from Buddy. All the deputies agreed this wasn't a rescue mission anymore; it was now a tactical bust.

Together, they changed their plan. Four deputies would now move on-foot to peak ridge to cover the Sheriff. Two task-force agents would accompany the Sheriff. The Sheriff would take his squad car and the agents would take the truck. Everyone else would stand by, overlooking from big 'M' Mountain. The Sheriff and his two agents got into their vehicles and headed to the mining office.

The Sheriff grabbed his radio while driving, "Buddy, are you there?"

"Yeah... I'm here, Sheriff. How can I help?" Buddy answered.

"I just want to say thank you, you've been a great help."

"Hey, what are buddies for," Buddy said. "Don't worry, everything is going to make sense really soon. You'll know what you need to know, when you need to know it, Sheriff. I promise."

"Ten-four, Buddy. I think I got a pretty good idea now. Thanks to you," the Sheriff said.

"Ten-four, Sheriff. Copy that... Buddy-out."

The Sheriff put his radio down and pulled into the parking spot area. He turned off the headlights and creeped as close to the miner's office as he could, without being detected. The truck, following him, did the same. When they finally parked, they all got out of their vehicles speedily without a sound. They pulled out their firearms and radioed for confirmation. Everyone was in place, it was go-time.

They crept into the backdoor of the miner's office quietly. Sharp and steady, they were ready for any interaction at any moment. They moved in formation, covering each other all the way into the payroll office.

In the payroll office, they saw a man emptying the safe. He was stuffing everything into his bags. He had two bags. One was full and zipped shut, the other was being filled. The safe was almost empty when the Sheriff and his men got into position to engage the robber.

"Freeze," the Sheriff shouted. "Get your hands up. Hands over your head."

"Don't shoot," the robber said. "You got me. I'm not armed." He slowly put his hands up on top of his head and he froze.

"Turn around, let me get a look at you. Slowly!" The Sheriff ordered.

The man turned around and showed the Sheriff his face, it was George Polsky. One of the mining companies' best electricians. George recently had an on-the-job accident and was medically discharged. A co-worker forgot to ground a hot-wire and the generator blew-up on George. His left leg was wounded, and he was medically deemed physically unfit to continue working.

This made no sense to the sheriff. George was covered by the company. 'Why would George rob the company?' He thought to himself. He knew George was a good guy. But nonetheless, George was caught red-handed in the act. The Sheriff had no choice, but to proceed.

"George, can I trust you?" the Sheriff asked George.

"Yes sir. Please... Just don't hurt me. I surrender... You got me," George said.

"O.K. Just stay still," he said to George. The Sheriff then turned to his agents and said, "Officers... Cuff-him, and put him in my car."

The agents did as the Sheriff ordered, and George cooperated. The sheriff radioed the rest of the team on Big 'M' Mountain and let them know that they had the suspect in custody. When they were about to bring George out, a deputy's voice came on the radio and said, "Sir, you're not going to believe this."

"What now?" The Sheriff said.

"You have got to come out here and see this for yourself," the Deputy said.

"On our way," the Sheriff replied. They brought George out, and the Sheriff's jaws dropped when he saw that back-up had arrived to deal with the protesters. All the resources the state had, were there in the tiny city of Butte, Montana. They immediately dispersed on the crowd and started making arrest. The crowd was scattering; the Calvary had arrived. They put George into the Sheriff's squad car. The Sheriff grabbed his radio. He told all his men to go assist and to help with the situation. So, they did what the Sheriff ordered.

The Sheriff got into his squad car. George was cuffed and detained in his back seat. The Sheriff looked back at George in the rearview mirror as he started to drive. "I'm only going to ask you once, George. Tell me, right now... Did you cause the power out?" He asked.

"Yes," George answered as he looked out the backseat window onto all the activity and chaos that was happening.

"Dammit George. What did you go and do that for?" The Sheriff shouted.

"Money... That's what I did it for," George answered.

"What do you mean money? The company took care of you, didn't they?" He asked.

"Yeah, right, they said they would. Apparently, there's a complicated process. That process can take years in courts. Until it's settled, I'm stuck. So, I'm a little upset if that's o.k. with you."

"Now I do understand that, and it does suck. That goes for everybody; even me, George. Why didn't you tell me? I would have helped you. Plenty of people round her would have helped you. Did you apply for a loan to cover you until it settles?" The sheriff asked.

George turned his head from the window and looked at the sheriff's staring eyes in the rearview mirror. George told the Sheriff, "That's it, sheriff. My loan was denied. Bad history, they said."

"I find that hard to believe," the Sheriff said. "Look, you were honest with me, so I give you my word, George. I'll see what I can do. But I must be honest, you're kind of in some deep trouble. I'm not going to sugar-coat it. Destruction of property, robbery, not to mention citing a riot."

"I don't care anymore. What do I really have to lose? I already lost it all," George Soured.

"Don't you talk like that, George. I'm going to investigate this. You can bet on that," the Sheriff stated.

George just shrugged his shoulders and looked back out the window. "Man, this protest is crazy," George said.

"Smart move, waiting on this madness to pull off your robbery. Now you'll be charged with citing a riot," Sheriff Haggis said.

"I had nothing to do with this. I didn't know this was going to happen," George replied.

"Wait, you had no idea this was happening tonight," The Sheriff asked.

"Why would I rob a miner's office on the night of a miner's protest? You think I wanted all that attention on the very place I was robbing, That's too much attention. I just wanted the cameras off," George said.

"Are you serious? This wasn't part of your diversion or escape plan?"

"You give me too much credit, Sheriff. I'm not this good... and you know it," George stated.

They both chuckled in giggles of laughter. The Sheriff pulled into the police station and assisted George out of the car. He took George into the station to be charged and booked. As George was about to go into lock-up, the Sheriff had one more thing to ask George. "Oh! One more thing, George. Who was your buddy on the radio?" He asked George.

George looked back at the Sheriff and said, "What radio." As the jailhouse staff closed the lock-up door.

The Sheriff's radio battery was dead. He decided to go back to his office, to get his back-up battery. On his way back to his office, he passed through the police station's main lobby. In the lobby was Mr. Biggs. He owned the First National Bank of Butte, Montana. The Sheriff looked at Mr. Biggs and asked, "What are you here for?"

Mr. Biggs stood up and said, "I'm here to report a robbery."

"What robbery," Sheriff Haggis asked.

"The bank robbery," Mr. Biggs stated. "In all this madness, someone wiped out the entire safe. Top to bottom… they got it all, Sheriff," Mr. Biggs Claimed.

Sheriff Haggis walked over to Mr. Biggs and asked him, "Well, Mr. Biggs, what do you know?"

Mr. Biggs replied, "I don't know anything. All I know is someone robbed the bank, emptied the safe, and spray-painted a message on the bank vault door."

"What's the message?" The Sheriff asked.

"See for yourself," Mr. Biggs said as he handed the Sheriff a picture. The picture was of the spray-painted bank vault door.

The sheriff froze pale as if he had seen a ghost. Goosebumps tingled his arms and legs. Chills came over the sheriff, as he looked at the picture of the spray-painted message on the bank vault door, reading '*Thanks for all the help, Buddy.*'

The Pool Hall

Jason's currency was low, and he needed to level up if he was going to take it to the next level. Nickel & dimming it at the entry-level tables would not make the cut at this stage. With only enough tender for one shot, one wager, one chance at opportunity; he entered the game floor to play. Shooter was his name, and his name succeeded him. He was a bronze player, no doubt, who had no fear of loss due to his well-balanced financial bankroll. The break salubriously fell into Jason's favor, and the game was now promptly to begin.

Jason aligned his cue stick for that perfect angle and determined the right amount of punch for a flawless break. Two balls in on the break. "Fantastic shot!" Shooter shouted as he clapped his hands four times with a smile that had hearts in his eyes.

"Thank you," Jason replied modestly as he prepared for his next shot. Looking at the table set-up, he would have to choose between solids or stripes to determine which choice was best. "Solids!" He called out, as he was now ready to play the game. They didn't have to call every shot in this game: only the eight-ball. Nevertheless, the rules state if you don't touch your ball (solids, in Jason's case) then it would be counted as a scratch. The opponent player can then place his cue ball wherever his preference be, on the table.

Jason dropped three balls into the pocket on his first go around. "Not bad," Shooter said as he stepped to the table. Shooter dropped four balls in his first round and Jason knew this gentleman was no joke now.

"That's impressive," Jason said confidently.

Shooter just smiled, but Jason could see all that poop behind his three smiles. He knew Shooter was taunting him. Jason rubbed his head as he thought to himself, *'Don't let this player get you down. Stay on your game and remember what you came for.'* Jason dropped every ball on the table in the second round: all but one. One solid ball stuck behind two of Shooter's striped balls, and Shooter knew it.

"You got this, *"wink, wink"*, Shooter shouted as he winked his eyes. Jason could see tear drops plunging out of Shooter's eyes as he laughed so hard, it made him cry. Jason's face turns red as fire in anger and rage of Shooter's humiliating taunting. Jason made sure Shooter saw his red face of rage. At that moment, Jason knew what he had to do.

A long game trick-shot was what Jason needed. A bank-shot off the corner wall to tap his ball out of that cornered trap and place the cue ball in its place. *'It was the perfect plan,'* Jason determined. Trapping the cue ball behind the striped balls. This would force his opponent to take the long shot with less percentage odds in his favor. *'He might make the first long shot, but then the cue ball will position itself and make it impossible to make the second,'* Jason conjured to himself. A defense strategy shot was necessary. Jason raised his eyebrow, as if a pondering curiosity came upon his face as he looked at Shooter. He knew he was mocking him. It was the perfect poker-face and Jason had a plan that Shooter was not aware of.

Jason could taste victory on his tongue and bet your bottom dollar that it tastes as good as that fried chicken he could smell coming from the kitchen. He could feel his cue stick up and down in his fingertips. Smooth it was, with the perfect slide and grip. He could see that prize money in his wallet already. He lined up the shot with every extreme precaution. Likewise, he pulled out his invisible mental ruler like his very own personal laser pointer, and he measured every angle.

It was a perfect shot. He hit his last solid ball out of that cornered trap and now the cue ball was accurately where he wanted it. Jason put his cool sunglasses on, and grinned at Shooter. '*Oh!*' Was the expression on Shooter's face as he tried to sink the first shot.

"Take your time," Jason said.

"I can do this all day," Shooter replied sarcastically.

Jason just looked at him and said simply, "Easy does it."

Shooter shrugged and ignored Jason's last remark as he lined up his next shot. Knowing he had taunted Jason; he would have to make this shot now or live with the consequences. Shooter lined it up and took the long shot. Just as Jason had planned, he made the first shot, but now he had no shot and was forced to pot the cue ball. Jason looked at shooter and said, "It was a great game." Shooter's face now turned red. Shooter had no fear, for he had a good bankroll. but Shooter had a little respect for Jason now. Still, he did not like to lose. Shooter potted the ball on the second shot, and now Jason would take his last stand with only two balls (both lined up perfectly) to finish the game.

Jason took his shot and sunk his last solid ball. Immediately, sad tears came over Shooter's face, and he knew it was game over. Jason, feeling overly over-confident was getting ready to take his final game winning shot when suddenly there was a loud roaring bang that shook the whole room. Followed by loud rumbling and cracking thunder. Lightning had just struck, and all the power went out. It was just Jason now, staring at the pool table in the dark. I heard Jason say, "Man! This app sucks!" As he stared at his iPhone dimming and flashing the words '*no connection*' across his screen. Jason knew his wage was now a forfeit by default.

<u>The End</u>

About the Author:

Todd R. Fabyanic was born May 22, 1979. Todd is currently attending Full Sail University for BFA in creative writing. He was published April 23, 2023 @ adelaidemagazine.org[1] for his first literary story called, The Pool Hall. Todd has written many flash fiction and short stories. He also writes film scripts for feature films, film shorts, and T.V. Todd specializes in the creative development of many ongoing projects. Many working professionals in the industry find working with Todd an exciting and productive experience. You will find Todd's writing works in Books, Films, T.V., Magazine's, Journalism, and many independent productions across the entertainment spectrum. The Flash Project: A Film Writer's Journey into Flash Fiction is Todd's first published E-Book. This project was a compilation of his college writings (both school and personal) assignments. The first edition author's publication was his first published release. Since, this book has been adapted and revised until graduation. No further adaptions or revisions were made after graduation, at which, this book became available for print.

For now, I leave you with a fantastic quote, '*Nothing last forever... So make today last as long as you can... While you still can.*'

<u>Todd Fabyanic (2023-2025)</u>

---

1. https://adelaidemagazine.org/2023/04/28/the-pool-hall-by-todd-fabyanic/